ANIMAL ACTS

Animal Acts

FICTIONS BY CRIS MAZZA

NEW YORK FICTION COLLECTIVE BOULDER

First Edition

Library of Congress Cataloging in Publication Data

Mazza, Cris.
Animal Acts: fictions / by Cris Mazza.—1st ed.

I. Title
PS3563.A988A84 1988 813:54—dc19 88-16487
ISBN: 0-932511-15-5
ISBN: 0-932511-16-3 (pbk.)

Published by Fiction Collective with support from the New York State Council on the Arts and BACA/The Brooklyn Arts Council.

Additional support provided by the Publications Center of the University of Colorado at Boulder, Brooklyn College, Illinois State University and Teachers & Writers Collaborative.

Grateful acknowledgment is also made to the Graduate School, the School of Arts and Sciences, and the President's Fund of the University of Colorado at Boulder.

Acknowledgment is made to the following publications in which these stories first appeared: *Indiana Review* for "Dead Dog" and "Erasable Ink"; *Fiction* for "At the Meat Counter"; *Kansas Quarterly* for "Animals Don't Think about It"; *Pulpsmith* for "Piano Lessons"; *Interstate* for "Shut Up"; *California Quarterly* for "From Hunger," published under the title "A Healthy Appetite."

Typeset by Fisher Composition, Inc.
Manufactured in the United States of America
Typography by Abe Lerner

To

MICHAEL AND TARA,

H.W., AND EVEN

HARRY

Contents

ANIMAL ACTS

At the Meat Counter

TODAY she's buying chicken legs. They have wrinkled yellow skin and bumps where each feather was plucked. He says yellow means the bird was healthy. Someday I'm going to scream at her. I'm not going to buy anything again today. I drop the package of meat I've chosen. I didn't notice until I dropped it—I had picked up beef heart. I don't know why I still shop here. I'll have crackers and a soda for supper. I'm going out at 5, then a guy's meeting me at my place around 9:30. I have to get up for work at 7, and have another date at noon. Most men at least say they like my smile. I wore braces for three years.

She tells the butcher he has the best legs in town. He says the loin roast isn't bad either. She's wearing pink stretch pants and a yellow T-shirt with a suit-case-sized purse over her arm. Her ass is huge too. My father probably still slaps my mother's behind sometimes, as some kind of joke. The butcher is talking while sharpening his cleaver. I feel ill.

This has been going on for a while, ever since I first saw her at the meat counter, the day after the last time I saw my father. She was smelling all the packages of ground beef. Then she laughed and hoisted her purse onto her shoulder and pointed with a sausage finger to a steak that was a little out of reach. "He likes it rare," she said to the butcher. "I stop cooking it when it's still the color of his face." The butcher held the package up next to his own red face. "I see you're a raw-meat man too," she said.

"And I'm a *big* eater," he answered.

"Watch it, I'm a married woman!" she laughed, "with kids!"

My father just called to invite me to dinner and talk this over. I said, "How can I eat over there . . . I'm a vegetarian and you can't endure a meal without meat." Neither of us said anything for a minute, then I hung up.

I was in the hospital with food poisoning again yesterday. I considered calling my boss's lawyer and suing that grocery store, but I haven't bought anything for a long time. Then I was trying to remember if my boss even has a lawyer. He would if he knows what's good for him. He was supposed to come over last night. I wonder how long he knocked on the door. Then when he got home he probably told his wife he decided not to work on his book that evening in the office after all. Or he could've said he finished a chapter and was so happy with it he thought he'd come home early and celebrate. He always calls her and says he's writing his book when he comes to my place. He works on his book twice a month, once a week *at the most*—I didn't mince words. I told him what I tell *everyone*—monogamy only pretends to exist, why take the trouble to pretend? *Some* people can't understand that. Why bother explaining—what more could I say? "*I'm* considering what's best for me *too,* Dad—I've decided what I want and what I'm willing to do to get it."

"You sound like a whore, young lady."

Maybe my boss found a whore last night. Once I told him I was going to call his wife back and tell her the truth. He said, "Whose side are you on, anyway?"

That's the trouble. There are more than two.

She shops the same time every day—I must be early. I've read the price on every package before she finally shows up. She walks like a pigeon, chest out, arms back. I've squeezed this package of chops so hard my fingers popped through the cellophane. I'm not hungry. I can't stay long. My boss is meeting me at home. She's choosing a rolled roast. "Getting rolled today, huh?" the butcher says.

"He's a real tiger, but I keep him satisfied."

Oh no—I have another date at 9. I almost forgot. I'll just tell my boss he'll have to hurry. See—it pays to be honest. I think my father's the one who taught me that. Somehow he's to blame.

Her purse is stuffed with green stamps. She's wearing a straight shift and flat sandals. She punches the price of the roast into her shopper's calculator. She keeps a stack of newspaper coupons between her ring and middle fingers. She has naturally rosy cheeks. Radiant health—that's also how my father describes my mother. Happy like this every damn time I've seen her. She needs to be slugged. I can't eat anything. Maybe I'll just stay home tonight. No, I can't.

Sometimes I take a nap after work, but today I can't sleep. I'm not hungry. I think I had a few peanuts at the Elbo Room last night. I remember—I told the guy beside me I was a housewife. He seemed a little embarrassed to bring me to his place because he had no curtains and there were dirty dishes piled in the sink and he drank out of jars instead of glasses. I just smiled. Maybe the way *she* would've smiled. My hands are a little red—so I might've washed his dishes.

"You don't *feel* like you've had children," he said.

"How many did I say I had?"

I got dizzy and collapsed and retched a few times without throwing anything up, and he kept saying "Oh wow!"

"The old man never got to you like this, huh?" he said.

"I'm living exactly the way my father wants me to," I said. He was sort of stupid. "Huh?" he said.

I ran all the way to the store, and it wasn't easy on these heels. My make-up took longer than usual. My hands were shaking.

"Sorry, no shrimp rolls today," the butcher says.

"Darn, and I had my mouth all set for them."

More than ever, I'd like to punch her in the nose. She's wearing sneakers and sweat pants.

"But," the butcher says smiling, "I have something better I've been saving for you."

"Naughty man—I have to be home in a half hour!"

"Just give me five minutes."

They're both laughing. It looks like he's holding a whole skinned cat by the hind legs.

"Oh—stewing rabbit!"

"Fresh."

"I haven't had any since I was a girl. My father raised rabbits in our back yard."

We had a swing—sanded so there weren't any splinters.

He's wrapping the cat in white paper. I'm still out of breath. The lights are flickering.

"You are what you eat," the butcher says.

"And you know what they say about rabbits."

"How many kids did you say you have?"

"Plenty! I don't want any more, thanks!"

"Okay, maybe next time. You try to have a nice day anyway."

"We will. My youngest daughter decided she wants to be a fireman, so we're going to visit the fire station this afternoon."

If I wasn't dizzy I might follow her. But I told someone I'd be at the Den later tonight. I might want to try that housewife routine with a biker. Am I too old to go to the firemen's academy? My father sells fire insurance, I think.

If I don't hurry, there won't be any bikers left for me. When I came home from the store, there was my boss ringing my bell, holding his briefcase and trying to see into my apartment, but I have a bookcase up against the window. So I knew I'd be late getting out tonight. As usual he would describe exactly what his mechanic did to his car at his last tune-up or repeat word-for-word the explanation he gave the barber for the kind of haircut he wanted. He's pretty fat and pulls his pants up too far and he kicks my clothes around on the floor but always folds his neatly.

Wrinkles are suspicious, he said. But I bet you never fold them at home, I said, don't lie. Good thing it's only once a week, tops. He knows because I told him I was keeping track.

I kissed him on the porch.

"That's a switch," he said. He came in and took off his tie. Instead of going into the bedroom, I sat on the couch, so he sat in the armchair. "What is it?" he said. "You seem worried. I noticed it in the office today too."

He put his briefcase neatly against the side of the chair. His briefcase has a little combination lock on it.

"It's my job," I said. "It's not getting me anywhere. I could go back to school and train for something better, but—" I slid off the couch, crawled on my knees to the chair and laid my face in his lap. He patted my hair and stroked my back. I started to cry. "I wanted to be a fireman—now it's too late, I'm too old."

He lifted me and we moved to the couch and sat there together. He kept his arm around me and we watched television for an hour or so. I went to sleep against his shoulder.

I fell asleep at work today. At least that's what it looked like. I think it was really a dead faint. My biker and I went from the Den to Sir Henry's last night. They have free chips and sour cream dip at Sir Henry's, and he was the only biker there. But afterwards I was sick at his place. I heard him washing out the toilet after I threw up. "You'd better stick to your husband and kids," he said. I braided his beard and put a bow in it.

She never brings any of her kids to the store with her. She's even wearing lipstick today and has a frizzy home permanent. "Big night tonight?" he says.

"*Every* night is big."

He laughs pretty loud. She's holding a package of halibut. "He reminded me last night," she says. "Today is Friday."

"I didn't think they did that anymore," the butcher says.

"Some still do. Habit."

"Like rhythm?"

"And we all know how well *that* works. But I'm not complaining."

"I've got pretty good rhythm myself," he says.

There they go giggling again. She's not going to talk about the fire station. I can see her underwear line beneath her skirt. I don't think I've ever seen underwear that large. She has a shopping cart but nothing in it yet except her sloppy worn-out purse, open, a fire hazard of receipts, stamps, lists, maps, but I don't see any photos. There should at least be pictures of the kids.

"The rabbit was delicious," she says. "I made it just the way he likes, and it was nice to be able to cook it without having to slaughter it first."

"Oh? So we have something else in common."

"Yes, I can commiserate with you," she says. "Sometimes I still have dreams about my father opening the belly and scooping out the guts with his bare hands."

My father took me to his insurance company once. His secretary was a middle-aged widow.

"What I'd like to know," the butcher says, "is how you stretched that one rabbit into a meal for your whole family. How many kids did you say you have?"

I took that pottery class instead of home economics, but I never became a sculptor either. Why don't I just hit her and get it over with.

"Oh," she says, picking up the fish and a package of ground beef. "You know kids—they only eat hot dogs and hamburgers."

I have to squat on the floor because I got light-headed, so I'm pretending to be getting a rock out of my shoe.

My boss sounds very concerned. I called to see if he was home. He asks if I'm feeling better.

"I'm going out in an hour or so."

"You ought to slow down," he says.

"Are you coming over?"

"Want me to?"

He looks different in a checkered shirt and jeans. But not so different. He fired the janitor today, a sweet old man, because he caught him reading the appointment calendar on the executive secretary's desk. Everyone in the office gave the boss the silent treatment, even me, especially me. His cheeks got pink and he sweat through the underarms of his sport coat. Imagine wanting to be stuck with him forever.

"What's wrong?" he asks. I don't answer, but hug him, burying my face against his chest. He pats my back but wants to get inside. He sits on the couch and pulls me down beside him. I swing both my legs over his and keep my arms around his neck. "What's the trouble?" he says. His voice is mushy. His hand is on my legs. His wedding ring is gaudy.

"I was proposed to last night."

"Marriage? That's wonderful."

I look at him a moment, then take my arms from around his neck. "No it's not." Why am I telling him this?

"Sweetheart. . . ." He brushes my hair from my face. "It'll be good for you, settle you down a little." He lifts my chin with an index finger. "You're not worried about *me* are you?" I am forced to look at his spongy face. His eyes are too small, his nose too small and too turned-up, his lips much too big and often look wet or greasy. I'm dizzy again. I nod and he suddenly pulls me close, whispering something, rocking me. I'm squashed up close to the nauseating odor of some kind of perfume and his sweat and something like bacon fat.

I've been brushing my hair all morning. I can hear it breaking—sounds like it's on fire. I couldn't go to work and had to cancel my lunch date. My arm is tired.

My boss called. He wants to come over after work to see how I'm feeling. I told him to make it around six because I'll be sleeping. I know that's his dinner hour with his wife and kids. He paused a moment, then said "Okay, baby."

"I'm not your baby," I said, and hung up.

I hung up on my father this morning too.

I'm going down to the fire station to watch them polish the chrome. Or maybe I should call and report a fire next door so I can see them drive up, lights flashing and sirens screaming—windows being broken, people jumping into nets, mouth-to-mouth resuscitation, smoke damage, panic, flames leaping roof to roof, axes hacking through my door. . . .

But why is my boss already here? I only got into bed for a few minutes to rest. He feels free to walk into my house and into my bedroom. "I called and there was no answer," he says. "I was worried."

"It's only four," I say. My voice is lower than his.

"Yes, I know. I wanted to come earlier than six."

"You mean you couldn't think of a good enough lie?"

He kicks some of my clothes aside and comes closer. "Your father called you at the office today."

"And you told him I was home sick?"

"You haven't been well for some time now. It's very obvious."

"Is that what you told him? Whose side are you on?"

He sits on the edge of the bed. I pull the sheet up under my chin. He says, "Got anything to eat in the house?"

"No."

"Want me to go to the store for you?"

"No! Get out!"

I shut my eyes and feel the tears on my cheeks, then hear him leave and softly close the door.

She's got a new outfit: a yellow and blue dress with stripes that spiral around her. She makes me dizzy.

She puts both hands against the edge of the bin

and leans forward, looking at the packages of meat. "What looks good today?" she says.

"How about some fresh octopus."

She laughs and shakes a finger at him.

Isn't that the ring-for-service bell? It can't be—I'm closest to it. Maybe I might've leaned against it by accident.

"Three of those chops would be nice."

"Just three?" The butcher smiles. "Kids having franks-and-beans tonight?"

"Maybe. . . ." Her voice trails away. The butcher stops smiling and stands looking at her like a dumb ox.

Then she grins and leans far over the counter to touch his arm. "Got any stewing beef hidden away in the back?"

He's smiling again too. "Wanna come back and test it?"

"Oh no!" She's laughing silently. "I'll test it right here."

"Okay, you asked for it!"

I'll be okay. I'm just cold—it's freezing in here. I wish I hadn't thrown away that flannel bathrobe my father gave me for my birthday.

The butcher is back. "This is how I test it," she says, picking up a cube of meat. She presses it against her cheek. "It's got to feel like the biggest, wettest kiss I've ever had."

"Maybe I've got something even better," he says.

She smiles, then says, "Actually I don't think I have the energy to make a stew."

"Having a rough day?"

"Just tired. I was at the hospital most of last night."

That bell is ringing again. Maybe it's the fire alarm. Maybe I'll move, find an apartment with a fireplace, a bigger kitchen, carpets.

"Anything serious?"

"Oh, it was just my father's pacemaker. It happens now and then. He's home again now."

"I know how rough that is—does he live near you?"

She stares at him. I'm kneeling, leaning against the counter, my cheek on the cold metal of the bin. "You could say that." She raises her chin and smiles. Her father didn't pay for braces. The lining of her coat is frayed. What good are nice clothes if you have to cover them with a coat. He brought my sweater to school and had it delivered to my classroom. I've got to have something to eat!

"Actually," she says, "my parents both live with me. Or rather, I live with them. They're both invalids."

"Wow, that's quite a job," he says. "Husband, kids, *and* sick parents."

"No husband," she continues smiling. "No kids. Just parents."

I've already torn open a package of lunch meat and stuffed a whole slice into my mouth. My chin is greasy. Damn her. Now I'll ruin my appetite. I wanted to call my boss and invite him to dinner at my parents' house. I'm right next to her dimpled elbow. I could touch her. Still at home, unmarried, and fat—what does her father think about *that*? Selfish old man.

Dead Dog

You Lizzie—you're in heat again. Another two weeks of this I suppose. A killer instinct: coupling and running in packs, the romance of being something wild . . . for a few days, at least. You're supposed to be a clean animal, that's what they said when I bought you, much cleaner than a dog. Clean personal habits, they said.

Years ago, when the family dog died in stud service, Lea dropped to her hands and knees on the cement driveway and threw a girlish-hysterical tantrum. But even after her mind resumed routine rationality—when she could think of the old dog and smile—her body continued to mourn. Her periods stopped for a year.

In those days, no law required leashes or fenced yards.

His job was to protect them: Lea and her brother and two sisters, and the house and parents. But whenever neither of them was busy—Lea with girl scouts or tennis practice or violin lessons, Laddy with personal affairs discreetly accomplished away from home—they spent a great deal of time alone together. Especially those evenings in late spring when the sky was still light after supper. Out on Valley View Lane, she batted a stale tennis ball with her old racket, and Laddy brought the ball back, damp with his saliva. All too soon the ball would be drenched, so it splatted when she hit it. (Then someone gave him a small green-plastic football which wouldn't get soggy. It was too big in the middle, so he carried it by one tip, in the side of his mouth, like a fat cigar.)

Soon his long dripping tongue would hang from the corner of his mouth, wet-red; and he would pant and lap water and fog the evening air with his breath. The sunset put an amber glow in his tri-colored coat, and a firey tint in his eyes.

At the end of every physical education class, Lea gathers the girls around her for a talk. She dresses every day in lean stretch pants, white blouse and a patterned pinafore. She keeps her uniforms at school, washes them in the school laundry with the towels because of the cat hairs at home. She believes it's a good idea to talk to the girls frankly once a day.

They meet in the dance room. The girls sit or lie on the mats there. After games of basketball or tennis, they fill the small room with hot dampness and the smell of socks. The mirrors fog slightly. On warm days the girls sit lifting their hair from their sticky necks.

"Basic hygiene," Lea says, "is so important—especially after exercise when the pores are open." She smiles. "When you wash you face, work away from problem areas. Otherwise, instead of removing the oil, you're distributing it." Lea's own face was never marked by blemishes; she's never needed make-up.

"Work the cloth down the sides of your nose and

out across each cheek. Rinse and wash from your chin downward to your neck."

The girls' breathing has regulated, and Lea knows it's not good for them to sit long in damp clothes, so she dismisses them to the showers.

She was never good enough for the first-string tennis team. She never made first-class scout. She didn't ever solo with the school orchestra. She was not abnormal, just average. She didn't date early, and she didn't date much, but she never said no—until her trouble after Laddy died. Laddy was a family dog but she called him hers.

She claps her hands softly. "Calm down, now, girls, take deep breaths. There now." She pauses. This is her favorite part of teaching. "I'm sure you all know how important it is to wear your bras while engaged in physical activities," she says. "It's equally important to exercise those special muscles which are always working to keep your busts from sagging." She puts her heels together. Standing above the girls, she clasps her hands in front of her own trim figure and holds her elbows high. "Like this, you see, each hand pushing against the other tightens those important muscles, keeping them fit to do their duties."

But no one could say she lacked the rhapsody of youth, even though she didn't read pulp nor watch much television. She danced alone to records, or lay down with an arm across Laddy, listening to Brahms or her favorite, Mendelssohn's "Songs without Words." Sometimes she held Laddy's front paws and made him stand up in front of her. She led, and he followed on rickety tiptoe, doing a two-step during a waltz.

She took Laddy on a backpack trip and hiked for miles on a wilderness trail. Laddy didn't stay at her heels, in her footsteps. He trotted ahead, stopping to look back every few yards, urging her to hurry, but his feet gave out before hers did. Lea had leather boots. She tried to carry him, but he struggled in her arms and wanted to walk. So she put socks on his feet. In the evenings by the fire, he licked between his pads while Lea hummed tunes from the Berlioz *Romeo and Juliet.* She offered to walk to the creek and bring him back a bowl of water, but he went with her, barefoot, and drank straight from the running river.

Laddy lived thirteen years, from the time she was six through eighteen. After he died, there was no point going camping alone. Or dancing either.

The girls troop into the dance room and flop onto the mats. Some open their top buttons and fan their sweaty chests.

"Why can't we play co-ed volleyball, Miss Palmquist?"

"Yeah, Miss Palmquist, it would be faster and more exercise."

Lea smiles. They need so much guidance. "Some things, girls, are best done without men." She kneels neatly, legs together, in order to be closer to their level, more intimate.

"The examination of your skin and hair is important, girls, because there are some personal conditions even a daily shower can't combat. For example

. . . well, body lice is one." Lea brushes her long, chestnut hair one hundred times twice a day—as soon as she gets to school in the morning, and right before she leaves.

"It's not as old-fashioned as you may think. Although in less civilized times it *was* more common, and our language was given words like lousy. But the condition is by no means extinct. Fleas which you may pick up from a family pet won't stay with you. But lice will. It'll itch, you might have a rash, but you'll seldom actually be able to see the creatures. You may believe you're just moody or irritable, but your body is telling you something."

Lea lets this sink in a moment while some of the girls squirm or look down at their knees until she sends them to the showers.

All the pups born on and around Valley View Lane carried resemblances to Laddy. He was gifted in that way—the bitches never refused, in fact, were glad he came calling when it was their time. Laddy was never one of those dogs caught stuck end-to-end with his bitch, looking sheepishly over their shoulders at each other, sometimes with a ring of people around them throwing stuff, trying to make them run away together or pop apart. Laddy was too smart, too discreet, and loved his bitches in private. So until his end—until they put him up for stud—Lea was only allowed to watch the courtship. He would trot directly to his bitch, panting his dog-smile, swishing his bush-tail. He had long enough hair to hide his privates: they didn't bob around in back under a puckered anus like on naked short-haired dogs. There was one of those on Valley View too; one tooth always showed outside his upper lip, and no one liked him much. Lea had been there when that naked dog had humped a bitch in the middle of the road, not even caring which end of her he mounted, head or tail. And he ran around unsheathed, his pointed tool red and shiny, and he drooled a lot, and wet on everything.

Laddy was more mature. Circling his bitch, he would sniff delicately, never poking his nose right in there under her tail for a taste. But he would lick her face, especially dog-kisses in her ears, and sometimes gently but firmly wash her closed eyes with his tongue. Lea would sit by the side of the road, poking sticks into the dust, rapt eyes on Laddy's impressive popularity, but she knew she would have to walk home alone because soon Laddy and the bitch would be on their way to his secret lair to enjoy each other. She imagined it to be shady, but warm, down in the weeds, in the canyon below Valley View, a sudden mat of grass hidden in the dry sage and tall yellow straw. A place she never saw, or may've seen and never knew it.

One time Lea had called to Laddy as he began to lead the bitch away, but instead of looking back, he had trotted faster.

Later, when he would come home, Lea ignored Laddy for a while, secretly watching him from the corner of one eye as he dozed on the porch, but she would always break down and go to him, kneel and roll him over to rub his belly. She loved it when he licked her ears, and sometimes, but not always, he would.

She calls them early from basketball in the gym. This gives her extra time for a delicate topic.

"The problem of cramps during the menstrual period is one we all have to deal with." Her smile is modest. She wants the girls to have clean thoughts about life.

She waits for them to stop shifting and looking at one another. Finally everyone is still; most of the girls look at the mats in front of their knees. Not a giggle. Lea is very successful at this.

"Nature's cure for cramps is to have a baby, but she provides no alternative until that time. There are, however, exercises you can do to alleviate the pressure on your womb." She holds onto the word, drawing it out like an endearment. Girls should learn to love their own bodies. Lea has taken excellent care of her own. "Lie thus." Lea reclines on the mats, sideways to the girls, knees bent, feet flat. "Put a book or board under your hips, tilting the angle of the uterus, then place two or three books on top of the abdomen, forcing the natural pressure to defuse and be absorbed. Also walking and lightly strenuous sports are by all means encouraged to relax and stretch the muscles there which otherwise will tend to fight back against the heavier load." Lea sits up, cross-legged.

"Also important during this special time is frequent washing. Not too hot or too cold, and girls—wash the outside of the orifice only, don't allow dangerous suds to enter your body."

Every girl's neck is bent, face turned toward the mat in front of herself, and Lea speaks to the tops of their heads. One girl looks up, squinting. They're listening, all right.

One afternoon after he'd come home from a private outing, Laddy lay on the porch quietly for several minutes and Lea was alone on the other end of the porch, sitting on a lawn chair with her feet tucked underneath herself. They were silent for a while, then Lea hummed a little tune, and Laddy opened his eyes and looked at her. So Lea got out of her chair and came to his end of the porch to kneel beside him. She continued humming and rolled him over to pat his belly where the long white hair was fairly thin and his pink skin showed beneath it. She rubbed him for a while there, then looked at his genitals. This was the only way she could see them, with Laddy on his back. She looked close. There was a knot, like a walnut, in the middle, halfway down. She thought immediately it must be a cancer, some strange tumor. But it hadn't been there last time she'd looked. She touched it. Laddy swallowed and looked away. Then she rubbed it, trying to rub it away or smooth the knot down into the rest of him. His body stiffened. His legs jerked a few times. When she realized it wasn't a cancer at all, she stopped rubbing it. She went away and came back in half an hour. He was sitting. She extended her palm to him, and he gave her a paw, as he'd been taught. So they shook hands. But then she dropped his foot and continued to offer her hand. Laddy put his nose close, reached out and just touched her palm with his tongue.

Lea blows her silver whistle. Her decision to stop their tennis games, to call them off the courts they shared with the boys and bring them into their own locker room, came when—for the third time that year—the coach asked her for a game of golf and lunch on Saturday. Instead of the usual answer, this time she blew her whistle.

In the dance room, waiting for the girls to check in their rackets, Lea thinks quickly, a fingertip against her lips. An important day for the girls.

"I've often said," she begins quietly, "that if I had a daughter your age and she had a boyfriend, I'd take her to the doctor for birth control pills. Now I'm not so sure—not due to any puritan reformation on my part, but a rethinking of what's best for a young girl. Birth control is important, and we can deal with it our own way."

At this point she sits, facing the semicircle of girls. "Well, God knows we all have our little itches, but really, who is the one who best knows how to scratch in exactly the right way? And what better birth control is there?" The girls are watching her; she knew they would, their interest is natural. "Above all, be comfortable with yourself and give yourself time. Be kind, gentle, and patient. Clip your fingernails beforehand, all of them on one hand or just one nail, depending on your favorite finger. Afterwards take a shower and wash. Sometimes it's even advisable to shower beforehand too, but in any case," Lea raises her index finger into the air, "be sure your hands are clean."

Okay, Lizzie, let me tell you something that might change your tune. When Laddy was an old guy, they tried to breed him with a dancing little bitch in her first heat. But they were afraid to let them go free, to Laddy's place—they actually thought someone else might do her. They said they had to be sure it was Laddy. So he and she had to be locked together in the smelly garage.

Everyone hoped it would be quick, without complications. Lea wasn't the last to talk to Laddy before he went into the garage. She had to watch through the window. He did try to nuzzle against the bitch, to calm her giddy anxiety. After all, it was her first time, and he understood. But she put her chest to the floor and wagged her little ass in the air, looking up at him, laughing. A few times he put just one paw on her back, but she slipped away, wanting to play; she was so young. Lea could barely see, everyone was jostling for window space. Then someone bumped against the door, and Laddy looked up and saw the faces pressed against the window. He looked around the garage with its dust-filled air and cloud of flies and open rafters, and he turned to the bitch and mounted her and humped, all business, and everyone watched, but the little bitch dropped her hips and wiggled away.

The stupid little bitch. So silly. Everyone decided to leave them alone, give them an hour. When I came back, there was Laddy: he'd crashed to the floor of the garage. I thought he was asleep. And she was still doing her dance all around him: such a tiny, silly, teasing, stupid, taunting, cruel, wretched creature.

She's on her way home, in the bus, exhausted but pleased with the day's work. The girls didn't even look at each other and smile today. Their school year is almost completed. The bus is crowded, but Lea has managed to get a seat, wedged between a couple of thickset older women, one with a newspaper, the other studying a romance novel. She doesn't read over their shoulders. In front of her, holding onto a strap, there is a middle-aged man with a briefcase and a suit box. One of his legs is shorter than the other and he wears a shoe with three inches of wood attached to the bottom to even him up. She catches him staring at her, but he doesn't quit staring just because he was caught. Lea looks away quickly; looks straight ahead again. His hand in his pocket is right in front of her eyes. She can see his wrist between the end of his coat sleeve and the edge of his pocket. His suit box and briefcase are held upright between his legs. His hand moves in his pocket. Becomes a fist. The pocket material is tight around it. She can see all four knuckles. The bus shakes and rumbles. The man holds his strap. Lea catches him staring and looks away. He rattles coins in his pocket, then removes his hand and straightens the suit box and briefcase slightly, so their edges line up evenly. His wood-bottomed shoe keeps slipping on the floor. The sound gives her chills. The bus lurches and the standing passengers fall toward the sides. The man braces himself with one hand on the window over Lea's head. She looks straight forward, her head tipped back slightly to avoid touching the front of his pants. His breath hits her scalp. Short, hard, quick breaths. She closes her eyes, putting herself back in the warm, damp dance room, telling the girls, *The best course of action in this case is to use your teeth,* hearing their guileless laughter amid lockers banging, the scream of her whistle in the empty gym.

Then everyone readjusts, shaking out crushed newspapers, straightening hair and clothing. One of the fat women leans over to retrieve her book from the floor. The man finally pushes himself upright again. Lea turns her face to the window, one hand holding the whistle that's clamped between her teeth. Then her hand falls, the whistle drops and she groans, "Oh, Laddy . . . what'll I tell them tomorrow?"

Erasable Ink

Sitting high on his stool at his drawing board, ankles hooked on the rungs, a straight smile with straight teeth, as though he had drawn himself: Michael Rixmann, a picture of authority, a man with a sex life.

He does, as a commercial artist, have the prerogative to draw people any way he'd like them. I'm doing that too, at second board: I've chosen him to be like. Someone told me to find Michael. A girl in the cab of a parked pickup truck. I couldn't do it, and she told me to be a man and if I didn't know what it meant, copy one. So I chose a man, like this: Open the refrigerator looking for something, I'll never choose a bottle of water. But take a trip to the ocean and I *look* at it.

Michael claims he's the one who makes the ocean rock. He says it when a lady walks past the window by his board: says he'd like to make the whole Pacific bounce. He lives on a boat which is where he controls the ocean.

I'm not really allowed, so far, to watch him do it. I may get it all wrong. But I try:

Start clean, then pull Michael's pants off. Don't leave them jumbled around his ankles which would cause embarrassing clumsiness if the phone rings, or the doorbell. Or if she pushes him backwards, he'll lose his balance. So I leave the pants thrown in a lower corner, one leg sticking out. He needs a girl so he can make the ocean have waves up and down the coast, a monsoon here and generous swells in Mexico. Someone who doesn't get seasick—but why should he care if she does? He's powerful. She bends over for him and points. She's *ask*ing. Then she's sorry she asked.

I know that's too short. But I'd better throw the paper away before Michael comes.

We talk while we work. It's an occupation made for talking. Otherwise we would have to concentrate on dressing lovely people in perfect clothes, or giving one lucky lady a new pair of rubber gloves. But this isn't really art, not like landscapes or massive seascapes, whitecapped peaks and mysterious green valleys.

He talks while watching his own board, glancing out the window, back down to his paper and swift pencils.

I use thick ink and strong strokes to make a single man: Michael's high cheeks without my freckles, his arching eyebrows and my eyes underneath—except brown, like his, but still *my* eyes, the ink is black but the eyes are brown. It's his hair curving over his brow, his straight nose without my tilt, his lips, his teeth, my mouth smiling his smile. Elsewhere I am hidden in one freckle near the corner of one eye. I tell him I have an idea: "Make me your partner and call us Michael Roberts Commercial Artists. You know, combine our names."

"You'll go on to better things than this, Rob."

"Sure."

He looks at his pencil. "Men who invented the pencil had funny ideas about themselves. Look at this." Holds the pencil up with thumb and forefinger like tweezers, measures with the other hand, thumb and finger, from lead tip to metal band. "Look, they figured we'd have this many great ideas, important decisions or new thoughts, and this many," pinches his measuring fingers to show the tiny quarter-inch of eraser, "mistakes."

"What about *ink*?"

A lady's outside—clacking clog shoes and Michael goes out the window eyes first.

"Two more hours and I'm going home to make waves in the marina."

"Alone?"

Hard white grin. "Maybe there'll be someone there waiting. The boat's not locked."

Oh yes the subtle excitement of a dark room and unlocked door, already uneasy with the water's movement, eyes probing, throwing their own invisible strands of light, feeling the way across the floor, hearing breathing, maybe his own, but too quick, and shallow, like panting, then the bed moves when he touches it—blankets have turned to flesh—sinks his hand or his knee into a soft body as he crawls onto his bunk, like sleeping in an anemone.

"That's scary, someone waiting in the dark."

And that, if written in pencil, would require using up a good portion of the eraser, maybe all of it. The quota of mistakes.

"You oughta try it." He doesn't say, *Wanna come try it?*

There used to be a closed club where boys could spit together, wear torn sneakers, complain about girls, discuss the sad state of the world.

The man on my paper is both of us: Michael Roberts, but smiling too shyly and lacking the bold anticipation of finding a lady in the dark. A mistake—in ink. Too late now. He glances up at Michael himself as he passes behind me to the coffee pot. Their eyes meet. I can tell. And Michael (behind me) moves on.

"I keep finding drawings which are awfully familiar. It's okay to practice—and to use me as a model if you need the practice--but let's not have any of them leave the studio." Pause, his back to the window, facing a wall of dull plaster. "It makes me queasy, Rob. Like seeing my face covering someone else's brain—a complete loss of authority over what appears to be me. That's an uncomfortable thought."

But it *is* comforting to be each other. He's back to his table, eyes to the window. I can tell every move without watching.

"Maybe you ought to try erasable ink. Have you seen those new pens?"

"I don't like ball points."

"Well, if you really think you need the practice, okay. But don't let your sketches leave the studio."

His only fear, naturally, being that outsiders or ladies might see. We crawled into a tree house on our gray knees, the dog barking below, wind in the branches. Close and comforting: And fear never existed. We showed each other our secret places which girls weren't allowed to look at.

And they're still not seeing my secret talent. They just don't want to, of course not, why would they want to be drawn upon, stained like pristine white paper angrily spattered with ink, then crumpled and discarded, no good for real art. But real paper hasn't a choice.

Erasable ink leaves smudges or traces of itself.

She's tall, a few freckles almost lost when the sun darkened her skin, a straight thin nose with no hook or flaring nostrils, hair to her waist, square at the ends, shorts and sandals and a beach bag for a purse and sunglasses on top of her head and round smooth hairless arms, vulnerable, like all of her. She lives at the beach, near the ocean water, tracks sand into the studio where it can get into ink and ruin pen tips.

"Are you coming home after work, Michael?"

"Home? Which home?" Audacious grin, boldly saying what it thinks.

"You know what I mean."

My stool squeaks. She's in the doorway and he's at the window and I'm in the middle, intent on my work.

Over my head: "How about we talk about it later?"

She answers, "Later, when I see you, we won't be talking."

He sits solidly on his stool. They hide the point while they talk, speak in a code only club members understand fully, he and she.

Yes, even a tall lady (tallness, of course, tending to be stately and genteel) doesn't act her usual tall way of not doing what she doesn't want to do, what she never should want to do—a good girl—shouldn't even want to talk about it. She should be scared of it. To him she said they won't just be talking. He made her say it, his slow voice stronger than a good girl's goodness or a tall girl's tallness. He actually makes her an ally—Michael and her—smiling knowingly together.

"Well, I'm the boss here," he says. "So I declare this to be 'after work' right now. Let's choose a home and go to it."

They leave, and leave the sand here, and the front door tinkles when it opens and again as it shuts.

His erasable ink pen is in his pencil box, mixed with other ball points, drafting tips, mechanical pencils, colored pencils, stubs, pencils with the eraser dug out of the metal band, mistakes all used up. Erasable ink doesn't flow, is lumpy and sticky and unreal, but a pen, any pen, is *my* only power. And from here I can see them, Michael and her: He holds her upper arm, her steps drag, she becomes heavy, approaching the wooden beach house. She lives there and is afraid. He holds tighter, pulls harder, has to take the key from her beach bag. She smiles, wan, her freckles stand out. I can count them (I'm close enough, watching). He tells her something I've heard him say before, "Sex is like business: even a little is good." Words on top of the paper. Geraniums in the plant boxes, red blooms, a welcome mat on the porch. She calls it home. Her hair becomes stringy and she is thinner. He hooks his arm around her from behind and she jack-knifes, her butt presses into his groin, he pulls her into the house but leaves the door open and the sun stares in.

She can be stripped in one motion. Clothes disappear but leave traces of themselves, lines across her shoulders from a bathing suit, a band across her waist where elastic dug in. Smudges on her skin, like bruises; she is very white underneath, like the whites in his eyes and his teeth in a grimace as he throws her to the bed on her back (knees up). She looks at him through her legs with smeared dark eyes.

He pauses for a breath. Knows what to do, has to make her wet. I'll have him use his fist, plunge up and down, her head is back, chin up, narrow and pointed to the sky, (her face is gone), her hands tangled in her hair, holding fistfuls. This is quick, I help him. It doesn't take long, she's a deep pond with marshy edges. His clothes have to go so I take them for him. She's afraid to look, knows what she'll see, he's a horse, she knows it, now she's finding out what it means, why she should've stayed good, she'll learn now, he has to hold her open, uses both hands, fingernails gripping, I give her all of it, in waves, my whole talent. Then free my hands to pull her up from the bed, her head hangs back farther, still no face, only her long neck and jaw and pointed chin. Carry her to the wall and put her back there and hold her ass up (her legs are useless), and pound and pound and open my mouth to roar like the surf as I break at the crest and she feels it like a tidal wave.

What would Michael say now? I've kept them both mute throughout. Is apology a requirement or just a good idea to be gracious and amiable after it's over, or is silence really more gallant? Gone this far, can't erase the whole scene. Erasable ink smears and leaves traces.

She looks through the studio window from the sidewalk and sees for herself that Michael's not in.

I'm drawing alone. I look up, look out the window and see her, but there's glass between us and a transparent picture of myself—snub nose, freckles, straw hair, sunburned ears—staring at her. She waves, titter of fingers, rings in the sun. She's headed around to the front door, the tinkle of the bell is her.

"Your name's Robby?"

"Yes. Sorry, Michael's not here, he—"

"Then I'll talk to you. I'm Dana."

We shake hands. I wipe on my pants first to get the ink off, and almost need to wipe again after her limp palm slips away, long fingers, painted nails, because it seems she's left something damp, not unpleasant, in my hand. Maybe she's been swimming. But it's hard to be subtle while pressing my palm down flat on my lap, yet I have to control the pen hand, don't want to splatter her, after all, she's real, a nice lady sitting on Michael's stool, crossing her legs, waving one at me, her toenails polished also, one strap of her lace top slips over her shoulder and she replaces it, smiling, flips her tawny hair behind her back. "Are you Michael's partner?"

"Apprentice." The word spits. A little drop sparkles on her knee and won't evaporate and she won't wipe it away. My hands stay folded in my lap, they have to, for control, can't even make myself claim I have to keep working so I can turn my back. She tips her neck to look at her watch, the neck and arms so similar. "You busy for lunch? Looks like Michael won't be back. Stood up again."

In the window behind her, I can see myself facing her. "I never eat."

Her mouth is like a kitten's when she laughs, red

and white and should be fairly harmless, juicy, quenching, I'm thirsty enough to lick the speck of saliva from her knee. Careful, be careful not to demand something (from a lady, probably a nice one) because she'll remain cool and sweatless and demure—although with laugh-slanting eyes and something not-pretty on her mind, some reason she has for flexing her leg like that, toe up, calf taut. Makes me breathe like an enemy. Doesn't she know? Mostly hers. My wet dream can turn into her nightmare.

"How do you survive?"

"I mean no lunch. Michael will come back."

"I'm sure he will. Eventually. What about now?"

Now I am rigid and prove it by not moving. How can she want to make me want this? Doesn't she know? My mouth suffers to lick her slick leg, to chew her up and spit her out, a blob of pulp on the floor for people to step over, for no one to be startled at, for someone to mop up. It's scary—what I'd do to her if I thought she meant it. Scarier because I can't, or I know the real me wouldn't. Michael Roberts would splash it on her like a man. He's not here. Neither is Michael Rixmann—functionally she belongs to him. Thick fast heartbeats between my legs warn me: It's like sinking the ship to lose control of my pen hand. All jurisdiction is ruined. I can't tell her she's nice. My crotch is telling her she isn't. And she won't stop smiling, smiling. It's not me, can't be me wanting to tear her apart into soft pieces.

Again her sleek arm arches beneath her chin, within reach. She lowers her slick eyes to the tiny watch face. "Oh well, I gotta run. Nice try, Robby."

Air avoids me. My fingers pulsate and I pant like

the loser of a race, or the winner, or the only one who ran.

Self-portrait: a sketch of possibilities. Two figures, just outlines, heads, trunks, arms, legs—nothing else (yet)—which is which—I don't know. Rob Hansen and Dana Whatever. Just me and her, the real me finally, or not quite, I haven't added any details: no freckles, shiny end of my round nose, tufts of hair standing like feathers in back. But yes, it's going to be me who'll know what to do with Dana when I finally supply her with gender: small breasts, thin ankles and sloping calves, black triangle, arms behind back (out of the way), bright dark eyes open watching *me* and my long, strong pen (erasable ink won't make mistakes), forcefully commanding the features I add, the dominating thick liquid coming sticky and uneven from the end. No mistake. Everyone stands still because I have to be careful not to confuse the details. Her sly smile goes on *her* face, the oh-so-boyish grin is mine. Straight nose is hers, the button is mine. Etc. I leave her freckles off. They were never very dark, something of mine she probably didn't want. We stand motionless while I tell her what I always planned for all of my ladies:

I wish you could enjoy it, but it's messy and I'll gurgle like I'm drowning.

Then I don't care anymore what she thinks. No matter what she's scared of, I go ahead anyway, the prerogative of power—she's crazy if she thinks I can stop now! Just stay still, Dana, and let me do it and get it over with so I can say I did it (in pictures of pictures).

Now—slick glow in my eye, massive authority in my hand, the expert, the inciter, the tip touches and

Caught, trapped, can't escape, almost framed, it's Michael, door blown open and the hysterical tinkle, and into the studio where he catches us naked on cream-colored paper, ruining it.

And I've drawn an extra man.

As soon as he's here, I no longer know what to do next with the girl whom I've forced to spread out, arms still behind her back (out of the picture), perhaps pressing her hands on an ache over her kidneys or clasping her fingers together back there, sweating, steaming, leaving stains on the cream-colored wall, while up front she now grins a terrible grin, all teeth, knowing, seeing suddenly and knowing that I don't know what to do next (and he watches) except perhaps I can give back her clothes, let her have a secret smile and return her arms which she uses to reach for—whom? I can't tell which man is which—can she? Can't tell which is me. A frightening orgy: not knowing which body is mine. Maybe all of them, maybe none. Probably none! Everyone except me having the power to get all they can, grabbing handfuls, more than they can gobble or carry away; and it's wasted, parts of people dripping, sloshing out of someone else's cupped hands as they run away with all they can get. It's scary. Scary! because I don't know what to do and I want to do it so badly and they've never let me become what I'm supposed to be, captain of my own ship, artist of the logbook entries; perhaps just as well since I don't know what to do or how to become something greater than how I look on paper, and. . . . But I started this. And I'm thick and artless with her—in front of him. For Michael, I'll put my pants back on, be the inciter (at least) of ending this before we're sorry. But which is me, which to put the pants on? They're both the same—how did I make this mistake? Too late to erase, he sees his own strong jaw, quick eye, confident mouth, two of each, we're the same and I can't put my pants on. Not such a comfort after all: a man's in a frenzy to get dressed and yet he's afraid (most of all) to end up clothed in a crowd of naked people. Don't know what to do. And I'm supposed to know. I buy expensive artist's pens (and he uses pencils).

Nice try, Robby.

Her inky eyes slant, her mouth a gash-grin, her long fingers point at me being watched by Michael and not knowing what comes next, with my dazed eyes moving from her to him and back again. Her tiny teeth show when she laughs, a cat's mouth, a yowl.

So I empty a fountain pen on her head (time to give up the erasable ink). Spread it around until she's gone, a dark place between Michael and me. Two men left—I'm looking at both—and Michael, over my shoulder, is looking too. Four of us. He reaches past me. "I'm afraid of this." Takes the ink bottle and pours it on our heads, first one then the other. It soaks in and runs off, down the board and into my lap. He retreats to his own board by the window, looking back now and then from under his brows, small sober mouth, no teeth, no smile, no other movement except his eyes flicking from my face to my legs where I'm wet and heavy. And I finally look down there too—at the stain on the front of my pants where everything spilled.

At Least He Didn't Play a Tuba

THE HOTEL in Cincinnati was slightly more than they'd wanted to pay, but it was only one night. His interview was early tomorrow morning, then he would fly home with a *yes* or *no* or *you'll hear from us.* The latter would mean waiting on pins and needles, but getting a *yes* would mean more packing and selling and address changing and closing accounts. Of course the *no* meant nothing more would change for a while.

There was already someone in the elevator. She was holding the door open for him as he turned away from the registration desk and picked up his bag. The elevator was across the lobby, so he started to hurry. "It's okay, I'll wait," she called.

"Thanks," he panted.

She smiled. Her lipstick was messy. So was her hair, but it looked like it was fixed that way on purpose, ratted and dyed red. The black roots were over two inches long. Her pants looked like long underwear, ending at her calves, flowers on a white background. She was wearing dirty nylon moonboots that went halfway up her leg. Her blouse wasn't dirty though. It was blue silk. She had about fifty plastic bracelets of different bright colors on each wrist and a seashell necklace which had been in style about ten years ago. Her earrings looked new—dangly sparkly red pieces of metal on one side, a long braided gold chain on the other.

"Where're you from?" she asked.

"San Diego."

"Oh! That's my home town too. Is it still smoggy there?"

"Smoggy?" He'd only lived there eight years. Maybe it was smoggy before that. "It changes pretty fast out there."

"Yeah, what part of town you live in?"

"North Park."

"Oh! I lived near there."

"Where, Hillcrest? Kensington?"

"Yeah, that's it."

The elevator stopped at his floor. The girl held the door open as he picked up his bag. "Thanks."

"Have a nice visit, okay?"

His room wasn't too far from the elevator. In fact, the doors hadn't closed before he was putting his key in the lock. "Here on business?" the girl asked. She was still in the elevator, holding the door open.

"In a way." Then he went into his room and shut the door. There was a television. He made sure it was working. Most of the channels were either news or cartoons. He left it on one of the cartoon channels. Sometimes if he watched part of a cartoon at home, Shelly would pause on her way through the living room and say, "Why're you watching *this*?" She was right because most of the cartoons these days were garbage. The animation was so lousy. But at least they had a television now. One of the first things to go from his old bachelor apartment was the black-and-white TV which they sold for $25 through the classified ads. They bought a color set last year. Just thirteen inches, but after all, five years ago he was a bum musician playing his flute in the park for dimes and quarters the tourists would toss into his case. At night his feet had ached behind the counter of a record store—the amplified rock music making him feel reckless, taking money from teen-agers without glancing at the titles of the albums they bought—to pay for that apartment he'd lived in with his cat. Shelly sometimes remembered it with him, laughing softly in the dark in their bed: How the cat hair was everywhere, even in drawers and closets, inches thick in the corners and imbedded in the carpet and sofa. The cat-box smell had pervaded the room too, soaking into the walls and the curtains which were clawed to ribbons. They'd let the cat live outdoors after they got married, but the last time they'd moved, it had gotten confused and didn't come home one morning.

Someone knocked on his door. "Who is it?"

"It's me."

"Do I know you?"

"You know, from the elevator."

"Oh." He opened the door.

"Hi." She walked into the room. "Listen, I have sort of a big problem and need some help, maybe you can help me?" She sat on the bed and crossed her legs.

"I don't think so," he said.

"No, really, it would just be a loan!" Her voice was that husky, always hoarse type. "Really, I have to pay a bill before tomorrow. Just twenty dollars and I'll pay you back, I promise."

"I have no money to give you."

"You travel without money?"

"No. I have no money to give you."

"Oh, *please*. No, really, I have to pay this bill by noon tomorrow, I really need it, it's just a loan, I'm good for it, I'll pay you back, I will!" She hadn't moved from the bed, hadn't uncrossed her legs. Her hands were folded in her lap. Some of her nails were long, polished red and sprinkled with gold glitter. Others were bitten off short and not polished, except a bit of leftover purple under her cuticles. Her nail polish was a different red than her lipstick which was a different red than her hair which was very different from the pale salmon-colored bedspread.

"I'm sorry, I can't give you any money."

"But *why*, oh please, you'd be helping me out so much, I'm really desperate, I thought you'd help me."

"Sorry, what can I say, I'm not giving you any money."

"But *why*, I'll pay you back, I *said* so."

"Sorry, I can't give you anything, I only have enough for myself. We budgeted carefully for this trip."

"Who's we?"

"My wife and I."

"So that's it. How's she gonna know?"

"That's not the point—"

"Isn't it?"

"Look, you'll have to leave now."

"No, oh please, listen, I promise I'll come back tomorrow and pay you back. Every cent. I will, I'm good on my word, I really am."

"I won't be here tomorrow."

"Then I'll come back tonight."

He went and held the door open for her but she remained sitting on the bed. "If you could get the money to pay me back tonight, why do you need me to give you anything?" he said. "Just go to wherever you were going to go to get the money to pay me back."

"Huh?"

"Never mind. Please leave, I'm going to take a nap."

"No, really, I can get some money from my old man but he won't be home until later, that's why I need it now, then I'll pay you back. Tomorrow. Or tonight if that's what you want."

"You won't need to pay me back because I'm not giving you anything." He was suddenly aware of two mice jabbering to each other in falsettos on the television, so he left the door open and went to change the channel. He found some news. The first thing he and Shelly had watched in color was a nature show on PBS. Well, it was a Sunday night, there hadn't been anything else on. The girl sighed and went to the door, scuffing her moonboots on the carpet.

"Have any kids?" she asked.

"No."

"Why not?"

"We're happy the way things are."

"Oh. Well I saw something in the park today. This lady was pushing her kid in a stroller, then decided the kid needed some exercise, so she lifts him out.

The kid wanted to hang onto the stroller and walk with it, you know, push it and walk behind, but she whacked his hands away. He was screaming and reaching for it, but she blocked him then folded the stroller and held it over her head so he couldn't reach it. She was saying Run, Danny, run! Isn't that a kick in the head? So why doesn't your old lady wanna have kids?"

"We both don't want any."

"You're spoiled, know that? That's why you won't help me. You were never poor, were you?"

"Sure I was. No one gave me handouts."

"'Cept your wife I bet."

"We worked together, okay? I'm not giving you any money. Goodbye. Nice meeting you."

"You don't need to lecture me to get a job 'cause I already got one. Babysitting. Pays dirt."

"Sorry." He closed the door, took a shower, washed his hair, then blow-dried it in the dressing area. He wasn't hungry because he'd eaten well on the plane, but they'd figured on that so he had only brought enough money for breakfast plus emergency cab fare in case there was no shuttle bus to the airport. He couldn't hear the television while drying his hair. When he came back into the main room a game show was starting. He was supposed to call Shelly so she'd know he'd arrived okay. He also reminded himself to leave a wake-up call with the desk clerk so he'd get up in time for his interview. Getting this new job would certainly complete his changed life. Shelly said he must've been the world's greatest bachelor. She even bragged to friends about how he used ketchup for spaghetti sauce and threw pots away instead of trying to wash them, and his dirty clothes actually rotted when he put off doing the laundry too long. And that happened more than *once.* He had to throw the bundles away and buy a bunch of new underwear and shirts. Besides that, the bathtub always had standing water in it—the plug hadn't ever really worked, but then got steadily worse. Shelly gasped, laughing, "I can't believe you stood in it to take a shower!" Now, every other week, it was his turn to clean the bathroom. She used to have to clean it a little more after he was done, but he'd learned and now he was as good as it as she was.

He changed the channel, then had to get dressed again or sit around in his underwear since he hadn't packed pajamas or a bathrobe. He used to have a sweatsuit that he wore a lot, on days off around his apartment. More sweat than suit, Shelly had said. She bought him a new one on their first Christmas, but he didn't wear it as often as he'd worn the other one. Suddenly he got a panicky feeling and looked around the room. His suitcase was in the dressing area, but— Then he remembered he hadn't brought his flute. This wasn't one of those audition trips he used to take the first few years he was married. They would spend $400 for him to fly across the country and play five minutes or less on a stage in an empty concert hall before someone in the dark house said "thank you," meaning no thanks, go on home, so home he went, and Shelly didn't even have to ask how he'd done when she met him at the airport. Walking toward her, he would see her eyes change from eagerness to something else. He couldn't tell. Sometimes she said "at least you tried," or "well, we're doing okay here." But he'd decided not to audition anymore. "Because it costs so much?" she asked. He wasn't sure what the real reason was, but that wasn't it, so they never talked about it again. He went into management at the record store. He still played his flute once a year at Christmas for Shelly's family party. Someone else played guitar and everyone sang along. The rest of the year his flute sat on a shelf in the closet. Shelly said she was glad he didn't play the tuba. She teased him a lot—they giggled in the dark before going to sleep almost every night. "The only reason I'm not selling it is 'cause it isn't worth much," he'd told her.

"I don't care if you sell it or not." She still had her job at a grocery store. "How much d'you think you *could* get?"

"Maybe a hundred. Not more than that. Probably less."

"You mean your flute isn't worth any more than that *car*?" She was actually flabbergasted.

After watching a few more shows, he got into bed, still thinking about that car. He'd only been in town a couple of months and hadn't met Shelly yet when he bought it. He'd gotten a check for playing with the city band in August. Then he'd been on a seven-day fast to clean out his system. He was lightheaded and felt ethereal from the whole ordeal, got the guy to knock fifty bucks off the marked $500 price because the car had no reverse. To go backwards he opened the door, put his foot on the ground and pushed *hard*. So that same day he used the whole leftover $50 on groceries at a health food store, but most of them rotted before he could use them. Fifty bucks buys a lot of vegetables. The refrigerator had still been stained inside and smelled bad when Shelly suggested he should escape from the dirty apartment rather than try to salvage anything. They lugged boxes of junk out to the sidewalk and held a sale. The leftovers went to the Salvation Army and the money was the start of their new checking account. They'd changed banks rather than try to figure out the mess his old account had fallen into. There were unbelievable sources of money. When they'd gotten their first apartment together, they picked through boxes of books and took a load to a used bookstore. After the guy decided which ones he would buy, Shelly said, "but would'ja take the rest for free?" They each already had a blender, so they sold his. It was crusted with food, but by the time Shelly cleaned it up, it looked better than hers and she almost decided to keep it. His high school ring had sold for enough to buy them each a silver wedding band. They'd also gotten a hundred for that car three years after he'd bought it. One of the last things to go from the old place was the metal music stand he'd borrowed while a college student. Shelly actually found someone who would pay $10 for it. Every month when the bank statement came in they were amazed and congratulated each other on how much they'd been able to save in just five years. Now the new job in a new city would mean another escape, this time from the two-bedroom brick house they rented—it even had a fireplace.

Someone knocked on the door. He was almost asleep, rolled over and heard the knock again. "Huh? Who is it?"

"It's me again!"

"Oh God, whadda you want?"

"Please open the door."

"Just tell me what you want, I'm in bed."

"I just wondered if you knew anyone else on the floor I could talk to. I'm not having any luck at all. Please, I really need help."

"Sorry."

"Please. . . ." Then she was quiet for a moment. He thought he heard her moonboots shuffling down the hall, but then she said, "Hey, you still awake?"

He didn't say anything.

"Hey!"

"What *now*?"

"I'm really desperate, please, can't you help me find someone else who could lend the money, please? You think I *like* doing this?" She knocked again, then the handle moved and the door started to open. Oh god*damn*, he hadn't locked the door! He jumped from the bed and threw his shoulder against the door, heard her grunt as the door pushed her back. But before he got it closed, she put all her weight into struggling to keep it open.

"Brat," she panted. "I'm sure glad my old man wasn't like you."

"Sorry." He couldn't get a good foothold on the rug, and didn't know why he'd said sorry.

"I mean my *ex* old man, you know?" She panted and groaned but didn't stop fighting with the door. "We get along great now. The rest was crap. Marriage. I'd rather beg money from a bum."

"I was sort of like a bum before I got married."

"So was my ex. And he's a bum *now* too." She

pounded on the door with one fist while pushing with her shoulder.

"He couldn't hack it, huh?" He was finally winning. She was strong but the door was almost shut.

"Wouldn't," she gasped.

Then the door clicked shut and he locked it, turned and leaned against it, catching his breath.

"Hey!" She pounded on the door right where his head was resting. "Aren't we from the same home town, San Francisco? Where's your loyalty to the old Golden Gate?" She pounded a little more. It sounded like she was using her head, then finally she stopped. He didn't hear anything else until she screamed "You're all bastards!" a little way down the hall.

Well, he was wide awake now anyway, so he got an outside line and dialed his home number. It was only seven o'clock in San Diego. Shelly answered after one ring. "Hi, honey!"

"I hate you," he said.

"What? Huh? Honey, is that you?"

"Yeah," he shouted. "Must be some interference on the line. I said I have to stay an extra day, okay?"

"But you haven't seen anyone yet, have you? How d'you know you have to stay, did they reschedule the appointment?"

"I'll tell you all about it. I have a fantastic story to tell you. You haven't sold my flute have you?"

"Why would I do that?"

"Good. Sorry I'm missing my day to clean the bathroom."

"Honey, are you okay?"

"I just got woke up suddenly, that's all." He hung up, lay down, lay awake for a few hours then finally got drowsy and slept through his interview appointment the next day.

Piano Lessons

James and I lost our virginity at 24. But not together. He found a fat and willing girl in a bar where he worked. And I began living with an enchanting vegetarian who was fluid and gentle, who understood my virginal anxiety, and best of all was not an expert or craftsman at what he was doing to me. He didn't have to be. Jason was like a gifted child who's given a chaste lump of clay to work with. His long hands gingerly coaxing and astonishing it until what he had was a unique and breathtaking piece of art, new every time he touched it, quivering and pristine, if not always beautiful. At that time, I was the clay.

We lay down together, I on my back and he on one hip beside me, his long legs tangled somewhere (with mine) far down the bed. His neck was made for my face: I pressed my eyes and nose against him there and smelled his earthy skin. But I was naked and wet parts of me were cold. It was summer and I shivered. My fists knotted the sheets, my toes clung to an imaginary pole like a parakeet perching. Everywhere he touched me he found an unpleasant, yet faltering resistance. My skin jumped and snapped under his hands. He moved his head. With his mouth to my ear, he said things, and his voice was warm air entering me, traveling through me, heating the cold, solid places and making me supple and comfortable for his hands to work pleasurably there.

It was a while before I summoned the courage to touch his penis. Softer than any skin I could imagine, and softer than feathers, and so like Jason in its flushed show of prowess and rosy afterglow, its fragility as it curled in sleep, dreadfully afraid of any harshness, without its own strength or armor, surviving on passion alone, and trust.

Meanwhile, James met and married Dina, a pear-shaped sculptor with my own name. Immediately I changed my name back to Nadine, offensive as *it* was. I accused James of marrying a pseudo-me, since after being his childhood sweetheart, I'd outgrown him. I hardly knew Dina, beyond her free mouth and flourishing hands. But Jason became more acquainted with her as he lent her a thousand dollars for something, and then took repayment in weekly piano lessons.

In Jason, Dina said, she had the elements of a master pianist, and she was going to refine the raw materials. We didn't even have a piano in our house. Jason had a plastic keyboard, which he tapped with his fingers, humming to himself. He hummed when he touched me too, tinkering on my skin with classical fingertips. He sang scales or études that never seemed to change. "Don't you learn anything new?" I asked.

"Plenty." He wasn't really moody as a struggling artist might be—not compared to James, who played keyboards and background vocals in a rock band and constantly had headaches after his rehearsals. James said the headaches he got during Jason's lessons were worse, though. Meekly, Jason would ask me to rub his neck and shoulders after piano lessons had made him achey and stiff. For a living, Jason sang in the opera. He was lovely and thin.

I have saved all the notes Dina sent home with Jason from piano lessons. They make a crisp little book, bound together, for leafing through on a Sunday evening, like a photo album or a novel. The first, titled "It Takes Time," simply reported that lessons would now last two hours a week, and that James would no longer be allowed to remain at home during Jason's lessons. James was awkward and gawky, his elbows and knees always looked raw and angry, but he had fuzzy gray-blue eyes, and he gazed over my head when he said, "I love her, but she'll never be satisfied with creating a piece of art unless the work of genius is actually her*self*." Their house was cluttered with decapitated or dismembered statuettes and awkward tilting urns with two necks or punched-in bodies.

I began packing Jason a lunch to take to his music lesson. Usually he wanted Swiss cheese and avocado sandwiches. Then he requested tuna. "Fish is okay for my diet," he said. He didn't smile, but sat sometimes staring at the keyboard without touching it. And on me, he often drummed his fingers. His delicate hands were never dirty, but sometimes left dim fingerprints.

The next note, only two weeks later, was titled, "A Drama in Real Life." Dina said Jason might often be late and James should stay with me until Jason came home. She didn't want interruptions and didn't want

James arriving home when he *thought* the lesson was supposed to be over. They were working on stage presence, groupies, and social diseases in the performing arts, she said. She was having all her calls transferred to my phone during the lesson. She said Jason should begin bringing roast beef sandwiches and use plenty of mayonnaise. Jason came home crying with that note pinned to his shirt pocket. He flopped into our chair and said he'd seen a dog run over in the street. We sat for a long time after James had left (shaking his head). I held Jason's hand and cradled his head. His lips were dark and puffy, especially in the middle where the point was swollen like a beak. He said it was a little brown dog, like chocolate, and none of the cars would stop. They mashed pieces and tufts of him up and down the road. I touched his soft, fat pout with my fingertips, surprised at how feverish he was. His tears crept over the back of my hand.

While Jason was at opera rehearsal the next day, James knocked on our door, sat in our chair with his head thrown back, and looked at me with eyes the chilled color of a foggy morning. I didn't go near him. After an hour I told him to go home. He said, "Dina, I can't believe you don't know."

"Dina is your wife," I answered.

Another note arrived the following week. The lesson had been three hours. I always cooked the entire time Jason was at a lesson. That day I'd prepared lentil soup, spinache quiche, potato knish, spaghetti with mushroom sauce, corn bread, avocado and cheese tacos and carrot juice. Jason handed me the note, then went into the bathroom and vomited.

Later, when I cleaned up after him, I found it all over, around the base of the toilet, spattered on the sink, *in* the bathtub. The note's title, "Seduced from Domesticity." The contents: "Jason will die without two lessons per week."

"I asked her last night," James said as he was leaving, "how she can tell Jason has so much talent." As always his gray-blue eyes looked over my head, around my ears, beyond me. "She said men keep their talent, if they have any, in the family jewels, and you have to try to get it from there."

"We have no jewels. Not even wedding rings."

"Balls, Nadine." And he left.

Jason went to bed and I froze his dinner. He held me in his sleep, his trembling lips pressed against the back of my neck. His muscles jerked. Many times during the night I woke to find an erection snug and secure against my back. I dozed serenely. He seldom woke at night, but once he did. He sat up. "Those things scare me in the dark."

"What things?"

"Those." He pointed to my shelf of binoculars. Without light they may've looked to him like a mountain range in silhouette or an uneven row of teeth.

"Why have them?" he said.

"For my bird watching."

"Well, *use* them."

He went back to sleep and didn't remember it in the morning.

Another note was called, "Made of Shit," and reported, in Dina's elegant handwriting, that I'd better start making the sandwiches out of a better grade of beef, or Jason wouldn't perform. She said to trim the fat and salt lightly, try cooking it one-half hour less. Jason's cells, she said, were changing content and composition.

"Are you eating that meat?" I asked him.

"No." He went and spent an hour on the toilet.

"Do you believe him?" James asked. He hadn't gone home yet.

"Yes."

Snorting, James grabbed my arm and vigorously marched me into the bedroom. Then he stood behind me, holding both of my shoulders, one in each of his hands, locking me in a vise. He pointed me toward my shelf of binoculars.

"Remember those? You used them when you were still Dina too. Why doncha use them again—Dina."

"Nadine."

"Yeah. Nadine." He left, slamming the door, shaking the house.

Jason wanted me to tell him stories before he went to sleep. I faced the wall, he cuddled up against my spine, and he sucked on my shoulder blade while I tried to think of anything. I made the stories up as I went along. Then he slept, drooling on my back. I reached around and felt the helpless loose lump in his underwear, soft and baggy, his downy limpness caused a tremor, like passion, in my heart.

The last note was next. James handed it over at the beginning of the lesson, instead of Jason bringing it at the end. He gave it to me, turned on the television, and sat down on the floor, staring above the screen at a place on the wall. There were brown fingerprints on the paper. "The Plot Thickens," was the title. "Jason won't come home for a while," she said. "He's made of clay now."

I began putting away my cookbooks.

"It's shit," James said. He put the note against his nose to smell it. "They're deceiving us. I can smell him on her. Slimy like clay between her legs."

I am a bird watcher, practiced and patient. So I let James take the two biggest binoculars, and I followed with my favorite, smaller, but able to focus more sharply, and he took me next door to Dina's house where an old man lived alone, sick in bed all the time, and we used his guest room. He never knew we were there. Sometimes he called, "Honey, is that you?"

Our equipment was sophisticated. I could hear Jason's voice when I watched through the binoculars. The focus knob also controlled volume. James and I kneeled at the windows, passing the glasses back and forth. He was grim. After he said, "See? They couldn't keep their hands off each other," he was silent. He sat all day with the binoculars resting on the window ledge. I wanted to comfort him. I should've. I looked sideways at his ear and wispy hair. He was balding. His throat worked up and down, I should've said something. There was no piano playing. Jason was naked. His lean, hairless back toward us, standing on a pedestal, his arms raised over his head, like two swan necks. And he was very brown, all over thick brown but with a wet sheen. He was made of clay.

Dina was standing to one side; she turned Jason's head toward her. She put a palm on either side of his neck, fingers up near his ears and on his jaw, and turned his head. Then she used her fingertips and smoothed the wrinkles she'd caused when twisting the clay. She licked each finger, then used them to stroke the creases on his neck.

"I want to stretch," he said.

She wet her hands in a pan of brown water, then rubbed her palms together, a slurpy sound. And after she'd rubbed his neck, his head turned by itself and kept his eyes on her, wherever she went in the room. His eyes, his once bottomless eyes, were the same flat brown color as the rest of him. She worked on them, spending an intricate hour with a small pointed stick, lowering his eyelids slightly, bringing his brows out to add depth. He said it hurt, but he didn't cry. Then she tipped his head a little more, and he had a fawning gaze. She'd made it, the large liquidy look of a brown-eyed puppy because his eyes had no white, and wherever she walked in the room, his head turned and his drooling look stayed fixed toward her.

His body never moved. It was hard for him to keep his adoring eyes on her when she went behind him. He said he felt silly, like an owl, and it hurt his back. So she didn't stand behind him to work back there. Again she wet her hands in the brown water. Then, standing in front of him, she kneeled, reached around and cupped his buttocks, one in each hand, remolding the already perfect tight form. His rump was small but not flat and always had amazed me with its white urgency. Of course with her, it was brown, and with her wet hands there I could hear the slick, sticky slurp. He moaned.

Dina's hands were like flower petals, I could tell, like feathers. They hardly made an impression except to make him wet and shiny in the places she stroked. Most of her hair had broken free of its clip, and it hung like rags. There was a brown smudge on one cheek and on her neck, and muddy brown on both thighs where she wiped her hands before redipping them in water. The brown of Jason was embedded in every line on her hands.

He said he was cold, and she said she would give every part of him special attention. I watched her work down from his butt to rub his thighs, still kneeling in front of him, adding more smudges to her face as she brushed against his loins.

She fashioned the tendons in his legs and the backs of his knees. Her hands flicked and fluttered brightly, pinching, poking, manipulating. Once or twice he giggled, being ticklish as he is.

He was chocolate brown and covered with her fingerprints. She tore no pieces away and also added none. She gave him no new form, but she gave the whole shape of him the subtle mold of her own hands.

After she was done with his ankles, she returned to the pan of water. Turning to reach for a towel, she slipped on the clay-spattered floor. She clawed for balance, shrieked once, and fell against him. I heard his heavy grunt, and he went over too, landing on his back, and flat. His butt and shoulders lost all contour. His arms turned to ribbons, a few fingers broke off, his neck lost endurance and his chin flopped to his breastbone. And Dina, she landed on her butt, on her soft avocado ass, sitting in Jason's tummy, sitting *in* it like a bowl because that's what happened when her butt bombarded him, separated his upper and lower halves, hollowed his belly and hips and probably obliterated his poor unguarded penis.

I streaked out of that old man's house in a second, and when James and I bashed through Dina's front door, she was just coming out of the studio room, quickly closing the door behind herself.

"What are you doing to him?" I screamed, or meant to scream, but panting, my voice was a rasp.

"He'll be okay. You have to leave him alone for a while. He's meditating on his life so far." She kept her butt to the door and her hands on the knob behind her. "James, what're you doing here."

"I live here."

"Not during Jason's lessons."

"His lessons never end anymore."

"Go live with Nadine—that's what you always wanted anyway."

"There's steam coming from under the door," I said.

"It's conditioning my clay and works-in-progress. Don't worry about him. He's in good hands. He's going to be a masterpiece."

"Not his own."

"You mean not *your* own?" Her eyes were small and hard. "No—the masterpiece will be mine."

From somewhere we all heard a whine. James looked wearily at the studio door. His eyes were sweaty. I remembered Jason crying jeweled tears over the little brown puppy smashed in the street.

Wanting to see better, as though the binoculars couldn't tell the truth, James bought a telescope and set it up in the old man's guest room. He moved a mattress in there and could get up any time at night and view the studio. The light didn't go off all night. Once Jason whimpered that he wanted to go home, and Dina snapped that they were already *this* far into it, and he should shut up and let her think. Her tongue glittered like a needle as she spoke. I had to trust her hands, though, she told him she'd make everything straight again, "like your prick always is," she said. "If it'd been soft as the rest of you just once, I wouldn't have you here, trapped as you think you are."

She obviously had never seen him asleep and vulnerable, his languid phallus needing to be pampered.

She scraped him up quickly enough. Before I got back to the binoculars, she had already scooped him up and piled him on the pedestal. There was a damp brown stain on the cold tile floor. A humidifier pumped steam near his base, and white clouds rose around him.

But I could still see him, shapeless, a blob of mud, not even five feet tall as she punched the air holes out and condensed him. He submitted meekly to her slapping and slugging. I could hear her palms smack against him, and my eyes watered, steaming my binoculars, blurring the scene for a moment.

She began slapping both sides of him with slightly cupped wet palms, easing the bumps and lumps. Then she held him and slipped her hands up and down the length of him. She molded his arms down flat against his sides, and gradually as her hands slid wetly up and down, his arms melted and blended into the rest of him.

"It was easier when you were already basically man

shaped," she told him. "I'm not good at realistic sculpture."

Which explains the way she made tea pots with five handles and no spout. No good for anything.

"She's wrecking him," I said to James.

"She's an artist," he said, "not a jack-hammer operator. And right now she's working with shit."

After that we kept to separate windows and didn't speak. At least not to each other. His window was often steamy and he cursed each time he had to stop watching to wipe the glass.

By morning she said, "Almost done, good as new," and Jason still had no arms nor legs or any notable features. Nor did it appear he would obtain any. He was a pillar, brown and slick, and his head at the top was just a dome. No neck or chin separated head from torso. She'd removed his large sensuous mouth, had blended it into the pole, and his pink ears were gone, and his nose—gone. But she did give him eyes, each one like a golf ball, or like tumors straining to break out of his skin. She spent a long time on his eyes, but they never looked different. She made dime-sized pupils in each, an astonished look coming from so slender a pillar. And once again, his eyes followed her. This time, however, when keeping his eyes on Dina, his whole body rotated, and as she walked to and fro, testing his eyes, I could see his only other featured appendage, a yard-long penis, erect and also continually pointed at her. She walked completely around him, and the phallus, without a quiver, followed her like a compass needle.

She said it needed more work, and she masturbated him with wet hands, polishing him, swirling a slimy finger around the knob at the end. Jason's voice rumbled from inside the clay body, the sound of rocks being grated to sand; I recognized his orgasmic cry, sounding like terror, building like pressure until the voice itself burst from the tip of the penis in guttural agony.

"Now you're ready for the show," Dina told him. She covered him with a damp cloth, keeping the clay wet and pliable. "This won't be like all the other cold, hard statues," she told him. "You'll always be supple, a new way to look at sculpture. I wish we had some of Nadine's roast beef sandwiches."

Jason's erection made the cloth bump out on one side.

"We need a title, don't we," she said. "Something arty and oblique, like say . . . *Love's Art,* or . . . *Deception,* . . . or maybe *Piano Lessons*. I like that one. *Piano Lessons* it is."

She pulled a rope attached to the pedestal, and it followed her, on little squeaky wheels, and Jason's erection, the lump under the sheet, swung around to point to Dina's back.

He won awards. The paper wouldn't print his picture because of the phallus, so they took a photograph of Dina and the brass nameplate mounted at Jason's base. James came to the show every day with Dina, clinging to her arm. Like the photographers, he never once looked at Jason. "Where's Jason?" he said to me, the first words since we'd taken sides in the old man's guest room. He wouldn't let go of Dina's arm. She and I smiled at each other. "Well, aren't you gonna congratulate Dina?" James asked me. "She pulled it off." Dina wrenched her arm away from him.

Every evening when the show closed, Dina covered Jason with the damp sheet and went home with James, who was once again allowed to live in his house. All night Jason's erection pointed to the door where Dina left, and in the morning it picked her up again and followed her throughout the day.

People paid attention to Jason. He was the main attraction. Often, if Dina was speaking to only one or two art critics or students, and a crowd gathered around Jason, she shouted, "Hey, over here!" Hesitant and confused, the people would, one by one, leave Jason to cluster around Dina.

"Told you," James said to me. "This was the goal of her whole little party with Jason. A crowd's ears and eyes. Where is Jason, anyway? This is her big moment; you'd think *he* would want to share it with her."

"Jason is here—" I tried to tell him.

"Yeah, and what are you swallowing now—that Jason turned into the necklace she's wearing, or maybe he's her underwear."

"You saw it happening—"

"I sure did. Every lurid detail. Where were *you*? I suppose I should feel sorry for you—we were fed the same shit—but you didn't hafta eat it and sit up begging for more. That's what maggots do, Nadine, whatever world they're living in, they *eat* it and are made out of it." James was not only balding—his face was lined, his mouth thin and sour. "So you can believe whatever about your precious shithead Jason.

Dina wants a divorce now. Some life. Welcome to the real world."

James didn't ever come back to the show. He left that day still gripping Dina's arm, more angry at me than at her.

I stayed all night with Jason. In the morning, I waited beside the chilly cloth which covered him. It smelled like dirt. There was a small rail around him, and brass signs saying, Do Not Touch, on all four sides. Every sign was dulled with fingerprints. Jason's cloth moved slightly, a shift in the air. I heard the doors of the gallery open, and Dina entered first and smiled. "Nadine," she said. "You see? I told you he'd be okay."

I said, "*Are* you okay, Jason?" I took the sheet off him while she snapped, "Don't. Be careful."

Jason was shivering. "Look, you put a crease on it, whipping the sheet off like that. Clod," Dina said. She went to smooth the little line on his trembling phallus. But as she reached for him with a finger and an inch-long fingernail, Jason's erection turned, his eyes, of course, following as the entire pillar rotated away from her. He looked at *me.* The shiny opaque brown sweated and dripped little muddy droplets around my feet.

"I knew these were a mistake," Dina said, flourishing a bright tool in her hand, and she sliced his eyes off, mashing each one in her fist, so when she opened her hand, his eyes were her fist prints, like turds. "There."

The erection quivered, began to bob and wobble. We watched in silence as it dipped, strained and yearned to be strong, but fell in gasps, drooped, wilted and lay flapping against the pillar, frail and timid.

Dina touched it with the toe of her shoe, nudging it. "Take him home," she said to me. "You know what to do with *that*. I don't."

We're at home now. Jason is with me on the bed. I've sucked every one of his white toes until he shrieks, pulling his knees to his chest and shaking his feet. I'm afraid one day he'll kick me in the face. Then we both calm and I hold his flaccid penis on the palm of my hand. The skin is loose and wrinkled. I hold it like a baby bird and touch the softness of the end, absolute silk, the unequivocally softest place in the world. It lies on my hand and trembles. Perhaps with fear for it is so unprotected, without a skeleton of its own. But I am gentle, cover and guard it with my warm tongue. It trusts me and rises against the roof of my mouth.

Jason touches my cheek and says, for the hundredth time, that he's sorry. "There's nothing I can say that'll make what I did right. I'm not proud of myself."

"It's okay, Jason," I say. "You were made of clay and therefore helpless."

"Why do you keep *saying* that—she made it up."

But I smile and look down at his penis, once again in my hand, but larger now. I push him backwards. He props himself up on his elbows and looks down his chest to his tummy where I've laid his organ. It is brown and smooth and slightly tacky, and I take the shaft between thumb and forefinger and break it off neatly, without pain or bleeding. Then wet each broken end with my mouth, that much I've learned, and mold it back together, smooth the crease away with one wet finger while he throws his head back, gasping. And the penis itself cries out with Jason's gentle voice, sharing his unintentional fear, yet trusting my tender power.

Animals Don't Think about It

It *isn't working very well anymore. She's starting to act like an amnesia victim—which she isn't.*

Once she wrote a biography for herself when an obscure magazine discovered her paintings. "Being both born and raised, Tara Katz now resides. The only one of her kind, she is in constant demand. She attends functions. Living with sculptor Phelan Barklay, her life remains."

She has the magazine—she must've written the portrait.

Lately she wonders if perhaps she could remember actually working on a painting—any of these paintings—would she like any of them? He enjoys them, while she can only dumbly stare at them or shake her head as he describes a painting that sold or one they gave away.

And they're starting to have the same conversation over and over.

"Tara, remember that time we—"

"I can't remember."

"But I've *told* you—"

All I can do is try to distract her . . . buy time . . . so I can figure out what to do.

His chessboard is glossy dark and light wood. He lines the wooden pieces up at their starting positions. "Look here," he says. He sits flat with legs outstretched, surrounding the chessboard on three sides, pulls it close to his crotch. "I want to show you the game I played last night."

Tara squats at the open end of the chessboard, facing Phelan.

"See, the opening is from the book." He reads the moves from his score sheet, advancing pieces, knocking off a few pawns. "Then I left the book moves as soon as possible. So I took this variation. It's not in any book."

"But I thought the moves in your books were discovered by grandmasters."

"So?"

"Don't you think if you memorized and used them for the whole game, you'd always win?"

"But Tara, this is so beautiful, just look at this, see, if he plays his knight to here, then I take, he takes, I take, he takes, I'm a piece down but lookit my position. See what I could've done?"

"Why didn't you do that?"

"Well, he didn't play that knight move. Instead he played here." Holding a bishop between thumb and forefinger, he clicks it against a pawn, pushing the pawn aside, placing the bishop on the pawn's square; and deftly, at the same time, he picks the pawn off the board between his middle and ring fingers.

"So I take this one here, then he takes, I take, takes, take and check. Now, if he moves his king to get out of check, I can go here, he pushes here to defend, I go here, check and win his queen."

"Then why didn't you do it?"

"See, back here, he interposed his knight to escape the check, so I went here instead. Now at this point, I'm still wondering if I shouldn't have moved my queen instead; let's see, if I go here, he takes there, I take, he takes, nope—I lose a pawn. Maybe I should've put this bishop here. Then when he takes, I take, he takes, I take, and I've traded a pawn for a knight. But will my end game be strong enough?"

He continues musing, continues thumping each particularly good move, or silently sliding the pieces on their felt bottoms for weak or defensive moves, then sharply clacking the captures. "And this would be mate."

She's undressed and waiting. Pulling him close, she kisses him, drinking from his wet mouth.

They slide easily together, made for each other. All he can say is her name, thickly, he cries and her name is his breath, his voice rising to screams, but always her name. His long white back arches, face to the ceiling, he calls to her hoarsely over and over until it's all out and he sags against her neck, still sobbing her name.

"Phelan." She rubs his shoulder. He slides off her, opens his eyes and smiles. "You feel okay?"

"Great. My nuts ache. I feel great."

"Will it be that way for me too?"

"It's hard for me to imagine what it would be like for you."

She watches a tear scarcely moving on his face until it finds a dip, a hollow, and it drops into his mouth. She presses her face against his, their eyelashes tangle, everything is blurry, his eye is a large murky puddle.

I almost wish I didn't know. Because I can't do anything about it for her. And I don't know what to do for myself.

She lies quietly looking around. They have many paintings on the walls with her mark in the corners. Phelan said she painted them. Sometimes a new one will show up and he'll say she hid it when she finished it, long ago, because she hated it.

He sits up to rub the cat who always seems to be purring or sleeping at the foot of the bed. The animal lifts its head, yawns, stretches. Phelan picks it up by its armpits and holds it in his lap.

Tara also sits up. "Why'd you neuter him?"

"For his own good."

"But isn't that why he's so lethargic?"

"I suppose, that's what I've heard."

"Poor beast." She touches him. "Doesn't know what's missing in his life, doesn't even know that something *is* missing. But what if he does. . . ."

"He doesn't care. No fighting. No late-night yowling."

"It's more than that," she says. "You know what I wonder?"

Phelan looks at her—a quick glance—then looks down at the cat again.

"I wonder what he thinks about. Does he ever wonder why he's living here on rugs and sheets instead of wild in the hills where he belongs."

"I doubt it. He belongs here."

"No, I mean, does he even know what being a cat *means*? If he knew, he might not *want* to lie around here all day doing nothing."

The cat purrs and rubs his head against Phelan's knuckles. "He's happy, he's content, what else does he need to know?"

Tara lies down again. "You know—I haven't painted anything for a long time."

"I know."

"Maybe I never did."

"Come on, Tara . . . you'll get over it."

"Think so?"

The cat yawns again and thumps onto the carpeted floor.

"Anyway," Phelan says, "he couldn't live in the hills."

"Why not? Throw him out there and see."

"He'd be back. He needs comfort and attention."

"Lazy selfish brat—doesn't even want to remember who he is."

"But he doesn't worry about it. It would be pretty hard to be as content and satisfied as he is if he worried about stuff like that."

"Who's worrying?"

It's worse than I thought. I don't know how much longer I can distract her.

After a while he gets up to clean the bed. He bundles the sheets into the laundry and takes out clean ones. None of their sheets are white. The pair he chooses have lions, tigers and leopards lying all over them. He makes the bed around and over Tara, pretending she's not there, feigning surprise to find such a large lump in the middle of his carefully spread sheets. Then she lies naked on the lions and tigers, while he goes to his workbench.

"Tara, I just saw someone looking through the window."

"Impossible—this is the second story."

"Maybe he climbed the tree."

"Why would anyone want to look in here?"

He grins at her. She gets up and puts on a robe.

"Let's go out and find him," Phelan says.

"Why?"

"Come on!"

They dress quickly; Phelan doesn't bother with underwear. "Let's go." He holds her hand and rushes downstairs and out the door. It's a clear summer night with a lopsided moon. They walk soft footed down the rural dirt road which serves their house from the old highway that's hardly used anymore. Both sides of the road are thick with semiarid shrubs: sage, wild oats, buckwheat, tumbleweeds, low trees, tall rubbery bushes that taste like licorice (Phelan cuts the stalks, peels them, and chews them for snacks); and a few taller trees: pepper and fig, like islands in the chaparral, left over from abandoned turn-of-the-century farms. Old equipment rusts beneath the waist-high vegetation.

Their house, which Phelan built, is much like old farm houses, but modified: huge picture windows in the upper story and a glass-enclosed belfry with a telescope. There are just two rooms: a combined bedroom and studio upstairs; a kitchen/living room downstairs, both floors large, square, uncluttered, without unnecessary furnishings. Phelan built the few tables and chairs they do have, also the bed.

Crickets and toads buzz. Their footsteps crunch softly in the sand. Sometimes the bushes rustle, rabbits run or sleeping birds nestle farther into darkness.

"There's no one out here," Tara says.

"There was," he says. "If all I wanted was to go for a walk, I wouldn't have to trick you." He stops and looks around. Tara moves close to his side, but as she does he suddenly drops to his knees and begins crawling into the bushes off the road.

"Phelan!" she calls.

"Come on, Tara, there's nobody around—let's play wild animals." He moves farther into the dark shrubs, so Tara also crawls on hands and knees into the bushes, but she doesn't follow Phelan. She can hear him rustling and breathing, but no more so than any other large animal stalking in the night.

So they creep around, growling, tossing pebbles—which rustle other bushes as decoys—circling each other until they meet, pounce and roll around ripping, snarling, flattening grass, crunching tumbleweeds, gathering burrs in their socks and shirts. Laughing, Tara is the first to gasp, "Help."

Phelan stands and pulls her to her feet, and they go home together and go to bed.

The room is dark; he is breathing softly. "Did you know you hold me like a stuffed bear when you sleep?" she asks.

But he is asleep.

She wakes once in the night, her arm thrown against his face, his lips pouting against her elbow. She moves her arm a little, but his mouth stays with her, clinging weakly like a tired anemone, weary of being fooled over and over by a finger.

He opens one amused eye.

"A suckermouth," she says.

He smiles against her arm and sleeps again.

He is so familiar.

She touches the palm of his hand and his fingers close around hers.

Turning away from him, her toes find virgin cold spots near the foot of the bed, sending whispering chills up her long legs. She settles onto her stomach, her arms beneath her, her hands going to sleep there, tingling numbness.

She says throw the cat out into the hills and see what would happen, but I already know—he would go find himself a new home and family.

Tara reaches to the side of Phelan's head to trace the inside of his ear, exploring. Her fingers buzz with waking up. She covers his ear with her palm, holds his head, edges closer, touches each of his quivering eyelids with the tip of her tongue, kisses him there, feeling the fragile shape of his eye, sucking gently. She puts her forehead against his, breathing his breath.

That's the admirable thing about the cat, knows just enough to love himself above all others and give himself what he wants and, beyond that, what he knows he needs . . .

I told her I'm going lion hunting. I'll leave in the morning before she wakes. I don't even own a gun. She'll be gone when I get back.

Making Things Happen

BEFORE THE BEGINNING

She'll always assume everything should be earth-shattering or heartbreaking.

At twenty-five Marla will always be on the verge of quitting her job as stage manager for a symphony orchestra.

At first she had presumed that her feverish organization of six men in coveralls, who set the stage, actually created the music. But after the concert, while she helps clear the stage, the musicians are the ones to go home with balmy content in their eyes.

She'll be allowed an assistant, Barry, a young, retired naval officer. He's been around the world; he doesn't show it. He spends most of his time practicing his French horn in one of the small rooms in the basement of the concert hall.

It won't be hard for Marla to know his routine: come to work, practice, go home. At first she doesn't care what he does at home. He reads books. Books which were already written.

Always too busy to read, Marla's time is occupied with pacing, gnawing her fingernails, screaming at idiotic mistakes and panting afterwards. To begin with she avoids Barry and lets him practice all day if he wants, finding no satisfaction or value in him.

IDEA

While Barry practices downstairs, a crew member will be rolling the grand piano onto the stage. The piano is mounted on a frame with wheels, moving so easily that one man can push it to the wide space behind the conductor's platform, where it will then be lowered on an elevator so it won't be noticeable or obtrusive until the soloist comes on stage. This time the elevator platform is already down, and as Marla screeches to stop! watch! stop pushing! the man grunts, huh? continues rolling the piano while looking over his shoulder to see what she wants, and next finds himself flat on his stomach on the stage, holding one piano leg and being dragged slowly forward as the piano sinks over the edge of the stage.

During this Marla will continue shrill barking, "The platform goes up first, first, first—that was what I said, do you ever listen, do you hear? Stupid jerk!" And the man, being pulled to the edge, glances up once, then releases the piano, puts his ear to the stage floor and enjoys the splintering, discordant finale, and silence. For a second, silence, until she flies to pieces, almost literally, saliva spraying in sparkling arcs and hair like wildfire, spewing her contents sky high. And it's Barry who appears like a wet blanket, leads her offstage to a dark place in the wings where he says, "Finished?"

"That's the trouble. I am."

"Did it help?"

Touching the frizzy permanent she gave to her straw-straight hair, "While it was happening. It seemed to. But it's over."

"I think you're fooling yourself."

"No. It *is* over." They'll have to be in past tense for a while now, until she gets another idea.

He led her downstairs to where his horn was still sitting on a chair in his practice room. "Let me tell you a story: I was officer of the deck one weekend, and three of the men with duty wanted to go ashore." He smiled. He has big white teeth. "Now these weren't your common skinny pimply sailors, these were brutes." Barry jumped onto two empty chairs, one foot on each, legs spread, arms spread, chest swelled. He made his eyes bulge, bared his teeth. "They surrounded me. One of them even straightened my tie while he told me in no uncertain terms what I'd been doing with my mother." He leaped lightly to the floor, turned to look back at where the brute had been standing. "But I didn't back up, held my ground and said—calmly—please resume your duties." He turned back to Marla, smiling.

"So what's the point?"

"That it worked." He seemed to shrink a little when he stopped smiling, perhaps he slumped. "Why don't you do your job without getting so excited."

"It's the only way I can get anything to happen, to exert—"

"No. You're letting *it* affect *you.* The influence is backwards."

"Maybe I'll quit."

"Is that the answer?" This seems to be a place he

should've smiled again, but he wouldn't. Both his arms limp at his sides, hands gentle and half curled. His face without a ripple of expression. Now and then his eyes might blink. Why hadn't she noticed before: it seems he'll always see her with his eyes, breathe silently through his nose, use his plain mouth for measured words, but something could be added—his face seems bloodless, nearly pointless, yes, and even boring! But to a musician, music is just black spots printed on white paper. What a treat he could be if aroused from this coma. And all the more delicious if she could have credit for effecting the sensation. If she could be the one to whet him . . . without delicacy, those same inert arms might seize her, the cool eyes might become volcanic and ignite her while the monotonous mouth will finally become a fire-eater.

"You mean, I should blow someone else up. You, for example."

"Well. . . ."

"C'mon, Barry, I'm talking about waking up your dull little world—"

"My life hasn't been dull."

"—sinking ships, riding whales, the rocket's-red-glare, bright storms in the black of night. . . ."

During this, Barry may stare at his instrument. His ears and cheeks are pale, his hair short, dark, his forehead white. His face has no lines.

LOOKING FORWARD

1

It will be time to test the response of the theater before the performance. I'll make Barry join me. ("It's your job too.")

So he'll put his horn away and we'll sit in fifteen dollar seats while the soundmen make sounds and the lightmen flash lights.

I'll ask him if he's ever tried making a decision which may not be his job to make, but inciting something at random just to see what it's like.

"Oh!" He'll sit forward, erect, on the edge of his seat, turning sideways so he can face me. "The commander had me bring the ship into Hong Kong once." I'll be flattened against my seat, deep in the red velvet. So he'll have to stand, lean against the row in front of me. "You've got to realize that Hong Kong has a tiny harbor, and this time there were several other ships there. Also they have only one way to get in—a narrow course between concrete buoys." His feet up on my armrests. "A ship has to stay within the buoys because the water is dangerously shallow in other areas. The point is, the buoys mark a twisty route, so I was steering that battleship like a sports car around hairpin turns. Imagine a bus making circles around a dime. That's how a battleship turns corners." A fist will make the buoy; his other hand flat, palm down, will be the battleship turning around it. "See, the person steering has to know when and how much to turn. I almost hit every one of them, I'll bet I had just inches to spare." He'll drop his hands, drop his feet and stand. "But the commander, standing right there, never reached over to grab the wheel." Sit, slump, story over, excitement gone.

"I don't mean following orders."

"Well, I'd never done it before."

"No, but did you ever rock the boat?"

"I didn't want to get seasick."

The soundmen will wave, meaning everything checks out and we can go.

2

So Barry is challenging material. He wants to be a navy story. He doesn't want to do anything unexpected. So I'll have to intrude and participate, that's the whole idea anyway. I'm not doing this for *his* sake. (And I don't mind the work; indeed, as long as I'm not in past tense, I know I've got everything delightful to look forward to.

He's downstairs again. I'll follow and catch him before he shuts the door. Light a cigarette and lean one shoulder against the doorway, eyelids half-lowered, wearing jeans and sneakers (I don't have time to change), but I'll wet my hair and slick it back and paste a few curls down on my forehead. "I don't know how to stand it, my roommate won't let me have men overnight."

He'll pick up his horn, mutely working the valves.

"It's hard to find places to screw—you know? How do you do it?"

While I speak, he'll blow silent air through the horn, fingering notes, following his music. Then he'll empty spit from the little holes and say, "I don't, if you want to know the truth. I stopped doing that after I got the clap in the navy. But that's another story." His sly grin will hide behind the mouthpiece.

"So how'd'ya get your rocks off?"

After removing several tubes from the instrument, he'll twirl the horn's body until water drips from each orifice. No longer smiling, "I usually just mind my own business and sometimes something happens."

"No!" Approach him and kick the chair. "I can never wait. I always have to *make* things happen. Otherwise everything that's going to happen hasn't happened yet." Then I'll return to the doorway, lean against it—this time with my back—hold the doorknob, put my feet against the door at the bottom, bending the toes of my tennis shoes up against it. And I'll pull on the doorknob as though straining to close it, but my body's braced there, my knees are locked, my toes push back against the door.

"Hah—I'll bet you can't, is that it?"

Rubbing grease on all the joints of his horn where the tubes fit together, his eyes will concentrate there to make sure he pulls or pushes each loop the proper distance so he can be in tune with himself, at least.

"Yeah, you poisoned your meat, it rotted, got rancid, maybe the maggots finished it off."

He'll pick up a rag to wipe water spots from the mirror finish of his horn—a tiny pulse bumping in his temple, a matching one, smaller yet, at the center of his upper lip. He'll blink occasionally, and there's the dull sound of his breathing. He might even sigh. A nice touch, but not what I'm after.

"And those guys were probably right—you screwed your mother, and that's where you caught the slime."

Barry will look up, dark eyes, sad patience there, even pity.

"No! Stop it!" Leap inside the room and let the door snap shut behind me.

As he is putting his horn down, I'll catch his hand, the one hanging between us. A shadow in Barry's dark eyes, as I stand frozen holding his hand with both of mine, his palm facing me like a policeman's halt. His hand, like his face, is unlined. I'll feel the harmless padded places between his fingers and tickle his palm, expecting it to curl in soft agony. But his hand can only mutely watch me like a face, stiffly upright at the end of his arm, like his own face there at the top of his stiff neck, pale and shadowy, eyelids lowered. I'll lean forward, but can't get past his arm, and his hand is so cool, nearly cold, and I'll release it.

3

Realism, then, obviously won't work anymore—not with an experienced reader like Barry.

"C'mon, Barry."

Holding tight to his covers, thrashing his legs—so I'll have to take him sheets-and-all, wrapped in pale blue rayon and barefoot with striped pajama cuffs showing at his white ankles. He won't even ask what I'm doing here. Instead, "What time is it?"

"Just the right time, Barry. I came over to get you, so you wouldn't miss it."

"Oh."

He won't even *ask*. I'll march him to the car. "You drive." I'll continue to give terse directions.

"The beach. What a surprise," he'll say, yawning.

We'll walk out the pier, Barry watching his feet. "Don't want to catch a fish hook."

"You'll miss the lunar shower." I'll walk with my head back. "They say there'll be a falling star every minute at least."

"Oh."

"I can imagine them falling into the ocean—*tssss*."

We'll reach the end of the pier and sit with legs dangling above the darkly vicious water. "Fire and water—battling to the death."

"Yeah."

"It would be something. Fire and water—they don't wait around. Think of riding a raft in flood waters through an inferno. Wouldn't that be great?"

"Not really." He'll pull his feet up onto the dock, covering them with his sheet. "We were fired on once, after the war was over, when we were pulling refugees out of Vietnam, and they were firing."

"Did you see any bombs blow up in midair?"

"I didn't look."

"Did they whistle before they exploded?"

"I didn't listen."

I'll count fifty-seven shooting stars in thirty minutes, Barry not even snoring as he sleeps, flat on his back in a blue sheet.

4

With a grand piano ready in the wings—one on each side of the stage—I'll tell Barry it's too early to set up for the concert, so he might as well practice a while on stage, to see what a real concert hall sounds like. So he'll be all alone in a chair on stage, and I'll begin to direct traffic, bringing on the pianos for the double-piano concerto, slowing one, speeding the other, carefully, using hand signals, urge with the fingers, slow with the palm. The men in coveralls doing the pushing won't even have to look up, faceless muscle, they seem to read me okay. Carefully, carefully. Then a simultaneous collision from both sides, Barry's horn shooting high into the air, his hands flailing and wood crunching, his chair splinters, pianos mashing into each other.

"Barry. . . ?" I'll slide on my belly on the black hood of one piano—creep headfirst up to the scene of the crime and look down into the thorny tangle of wood. "Bare—rey . . . where *are* you. . . ?"

"Wha'did you do now?" Here he comes, walking out of the wings. "How'd you get these pianos here by yourself?" Now crossing the stage, limping only slightly.

5

Barry will be raising the elevator platform from the orchestra pit, riding it up, standing in the middle with a stack of chairs he's bringing up to the stage. One hand on the chairs, the other in his pocket, playing with loose change. I'll lie flat on the stage, ready for him. He isn't looking yet. I'll unfold the picture, ripped from a magazine: the cameraman must've been between the girl's legs, a close-up. In the background, her angelic face, pursed red mouth, half-closed eyes. I'll hold the picture open over the edge of the stage.

"Barry."

He'll turn and stare right into her, the elevator continuing its ascent, and Barry's face will break through the picture.

"I can get her for you."

He'll continue to rise. I'll have to kneel, then stand, keeping our faces inches apart, until his head is above me again.

"Say something!"

"Waste of paper."

6

All I want is to get to the end of the future tense. I'll convince one of the musicians to be sick, allowing

Barry to perform at the special outdoor concert in the football stadium. Naturally, he'll have to inform me that he won't be working crew that night.

Then I'll plop down on my butt on the empty stage floor and bawl hot tears. "I need you—I can't do everything alone."

He's supposed to kneel beside me and push my matted hair aside.

"Did I ever tell you about the time the commander was ill and taken ashore, and I was left commanding half the crew in the tail of a hurricane?"

"Yes. Probably." The tears cease. Lighting matches close to my head, I'll begin burning curls, one by one.

"This wasn't just wind and rain. We had to hold onto things so we wouldn't be blown overboard."

Hold a curl in thumb and forefinger, inches from my scalp, light it and let it burn up to my fingers.

"And the rain was really like waves washing over the ship. There probably were real waves too, but I'm sure just as much water came from the sky as from the ocean. The deck was awash."

I'll begin singeing my eyelashes, holding the match near my eyeballs.

"Times like that are what the regulation book was written for. I knew it, the crew knew it. I never had to raise my voice or give an order twice. I never had to take the wheel myself."

Still holding a match at eye level, I'll look at him through the flame. His face is shiny, synthetic—I can't see the pores—this dust jacket actually tells the truth: he's not *in* that storm, he's in stories about it, black-and-white navy stories in past tense. Slowly sinking backwards onto the stage floor, blinking up at the dead lights, the spider web of ropes, the used and discarded backdrops, I'll realize if his story's already been told, if it's already over, I can't use him.

7

I'll have to arrive early at the football stadium, overseeing the assembly of the stage and shell, as well as watching the fireworks preparation, telling them where to set up and seeing that it's roped off.

"But lady, you don't know nothing about fireworks."

"I don't care. You just set up and wait for the lights to go out."

Trucks will arrive with symphony chairs, music stands, tables for the backstage areas, microphones and lights and speakers and portable curtains to hide the backstage tables, portable toilets, (all on a checklist on my clipboard), a podium, a piano, percussion instruments, a harp and protective harpist; the coffee maker will arrive by van with a cardboard box of cups and spoons, lumpy creamer and hardened sugar. There's a motor home that will drive backstage, park, and become VIP dressing rooms, ropes everywhere, and the audience will be arriving steadily, spreading blankets on the football grass and picnicking, while the crew wires the stage with the microphones and mounts speakers on scaffolding. I will be pacing, clipboard in the crook of one arm, mid-length dark skirt with splashes of red, pointing, screaming, hardly aware that once Barry steered a crew of a thousand eighteen-year-old sailors through a monsoon. The fireworks men in their white coveralls will sit and smoke in their circle of rope, waiting to push the buttons and go home, grinning every time I swish past, shrieking. Now musicians will begin to arrive, cool and fresh from afternoon naps and lovemaking. They'll pile their cases on the tables backstage and go for coffee and hot dogs. Barry will be immaculate and grand in black tails, white tie, his silver horn gleaming, his hair wet and combed, solemnly unexcited, suave and demure and playing the role he's practiced for. But with my hair and blouse streaked with furious sweat, I'll jump him at his car and trail him into the backstage area. I know it's no good anymore, I should quit. But it's just so hard to drop him, to simply give him up after this much effort and anticipation. Following him, I'm going to grab his tails and rip the seam up his back—just to make him look, at least. But I can't catch up, he's just out of reach, can't feel my frantic hand behind him, grabbing nothing. If I stop now and stand still: without hurry, without urgency, he'll simply dissolve.

FINALLY

Squatting in the wings, Marla will watch the last of the musicians flip his tails up and sit. Aware of the audience, even during preconcert warm-up, they are professionally calm, nearly bored. But especially Barry: playing his part. He knows it so well. He's practiced so much. This will just be the retelling of an old story unless she's clever and quick. Taking her matches and dropping to her knees, she'll crawl between the feet and chairs and music stands to a position behind Barry's chair. She can reach underneath to his shoes. Navy shoes. The lighted match at the end of her arm will lick at his laces. But they're synthetic and won't easily ignite, so the match will burn down to her fingers.

Time's running out. The conductor will be on soon. The music will be read from books, nothing unexpected, all according to plan. But she'll never let the musicians—with their big salaries and short hours—fool her. The stage manager runs the show.

Turning toward the light booth—far up in the bleachers—she'll start slowly, then run, then bolt through the people in the stands—picnicking, clapping, laughing, singing along. She loses her shoes through the gaps under the benches. Air is sharp in her chest, and she breathes with an open mouth to get all she can. Her head fills like a balloon, the sky spins, she pants in spasms, her fists open and close. She reaches the top and wants to go on, fly from the bleachers into the stars, sent up in a volcanic spray, out of the world. But this has to be dignified and spectacular, so she breaks into the light booth, reaches past the man there and kills the lights: all the lights overhead and the spotlights, all the power in the microphones and speakers and the motor home hookup where the television goes off in the dressing room. The fireworks men leap from their seats, and the first red and blue explosions paint the sky.

Outside the light booth, Marla greets her fireworks with breathless chill, and she pauses there before descending. Closer to the ground, rockets with white tails hiss, then destroy themselves in bright-white explosions. Meanwhile overhead, an ensemble of color splashes and falls from the sky. Barefoot, Marla walks through the grass backstage, her head tilted back, mouth open. The ash settles in her hair. One after another each bomb whistles into the sky and bursts into fragments, which hesitate there and glitter, raining color, sparks and flame. Very close overhead, many seem like shimmering umbrellas right over the stage. The musicians wrap their coats around their instruments as the ash swirls thicker. The audience is silent, and the sound is enormous as the sky seems to ignite, catch flame, and pieces of burning color fall out of the stars, land and sizzle in the grass. The rockets leave smoldering holes in the shell and curtains, stars of fire explode at eye level, spitting bright flecks. Sparks of yellow and green, red and glimmering blue fill the air like haze. Marla clasps her hands and curls her toes as sparks splash like glittering waves around her ankles, tingling bright and hot against her legs and feet. Several wooden instruments are on fire, blue flames peek and bob from the holes in the cellos, and flames crackle in the curtains. The musicians use music stands for shields and join the fleeing audience and crew and even the fireworks men, all seeking shelter under the bleachers. But Barry, running without his horn, does stop. He looks around, shouting something which could be "All hands on deck." Why not? But a silver rocket plasters him, sends him headfirst through the curtains, and he runs with the seat of his trousers burning, while Marla wanders onto the empty stage, gripping her chilly arms, looking up, looking around. A piece of falling fire hits a box of fireworks, creating a final gusher of colored flame fifty yards into the air like an exotic fountain. The stage burns amid a tempest of arcing rainbows. Marla catches her breath. She's left alone to bring the house down. She stays cackling with the flames in delight. She presumes—during the moment she has it—she'll always be riding the crest of a wave of colored fire.

FINISHED

It was over. She kicked through the burned rubble, but didn't take anything. It wouldn't burn again. Past tense is the worst. She knew she had to start all over some other place, which is not at all the same as quitting. Because she *will* go back to a different beginning to make something else. It's the desire that always rekindles.

Nervous Dog

THEY said you don't work here anymore, so I asked if I could have your job. I was joking. You know that. Did you leave this plant on the desk? It's dead now. Any of these pencils in the drawer could be yours too, the bite marks might be an impression of your teeth. So typical of us—you chewed pencils and I bit my nails. You bit *me* once too. I forget why. I forgive you, though. They've moved your desk out from the corner where you liked it. The safe soft chair has been replaced by a backless stool on wheels. Is that why you left? I can tell you firsthand it isn't very comfortable. My butt is already sore. When I asked if I could leave a message for you, they looked at each other and shrugged, and your desk was empty and your typewriter free, so they shrugged again when I asked to borrow it to write the message they said I could leave. I wanted to know if you remembered or ever thought about the last time you saw me. (You know, our big reunion.) Has it been a year now? I was going to ask you, remind you what happened, see what you thought about it now. How much time will have to pass before it becomes funny? You could tell your grandkids—whoops, sorry about that, my mistake. You know, clumsy me. They keep interrupting me, saying they don't think you'll ever be back, that you quit last year. They've probably read all the messages I've ever left for you. Don't worry, this time I'll change all the important details, and most of the unimportant ones too. I'll fix it so no one else could possibly recognize you. But I wish I wouldn't have to—so that if you came back from lunch or a coffee break right now, we could just look at each other, and we'd already know what happened. I'm sorry about your dog. That much I would have to say out loud. But I wouldn't have to go through the rest of this—every detail, word-for-word, just so they can pass it around the bank later. Some of them will assume it's all true and others will think none of it could possibly be true. But *you'll* know.

I wonder what your first thought was when you first caught sight of me, right before you slammed on your brakes. It was raining and I was cold and I'd forgotten which house was yours. (After all, it'd been three years since I'd been there.) But maybe I'd better sort of rephrase that—I was in a bicycle accident and was lying in the street, tangled in my spokes, blood coming from my mouth and nose, so you took me home. Of course *I* couldn't talk, not right at first, but you could've, if you wanted, but you didn't. Not even *Hi,* or *Long-time-no-see,* or *My God it's good to see you again,* or *I've been devastated since I kicked you out.* (That would've been nice. In a way.) Maybe you said, "This again," but I couldn't tell. By that time I was up to my ears in strawberry bubble bath and you had your back turned, reaching for a washcloth and soap. I don't know what you meant—you'd never given me a bubble bath before. Is that what a baby feels like?

You gently washed me all over, every cut and scrape, every bruise, every aching muscle. You should've been a doctor. Didn't I used to tell you that?

Then the dog started to whimper, and you said, "Just a minute." That might've been the first thing you said, if you didn't say, "This again," unless you whispered something about regretting something as you drove me home with my head in your lap. I didn't know it was a dog at first. The sound was what you'd expect to come from a baby deer—in an ecology movie—who'd been hit by a car or wounded by a hunter, but, come to think of it, they don't make any sounds, do they? Remember that deer I saw when we went camping? You made so much noise getting your camera out, it ran away before you ever saw it. You almost cried. It's probably too late to congratulate you now for not crying that time.

I caught a glimpse of the dog as you carried it to the back yard. A little poodle, white, with soft curly hair and runny eyes. Remind you of anyone you know? Well, anyway, when you came back to the bathroom I said, "When did you get a dog? Can I see it? Is he friendly? Let's take it to the park or the beach on Sunday!"

You shook your head and said, "No."

"What? Did you say *no*? Why? Why not?"

"It wouldn't do any good."

That's what you said. I said, "What the hell—"

"It can't change anything." Your voice started that familiar watery wobble. I knew it was time for a different subject.

"Are you still working in the yogurt factory?" It would be fun to change that and say that you worked for the government, testing new synthetic food on rats, but that you always felt sorry for them and ate most of the samples yourself. But that would sort of be classified information. You would never tell me what you'd eaten all day. Anyway, everyone knows what you really did, so I'll say you were a vacuum cleaner salesperson, but I asked you if you worked in a yogurt factory because you always liked yogurt, and *I'd* worked in a yogurt factory once, wallowing for eight hours up to my ankles in yogurt, and I can't stand the stuff. Looks like goat vomit. That was before I'd become a first-grade teacher, but maybe I'd better change that too—people might not want to know these things about teachers. So let's say I was an athlete, maybe a bike racer, that's why I was on a bike when I had the accident right before you found me. But anyway, that's what people always ask each other when they haven't seen each other for three years: *What do you do now?* instead of *Who are you now?* What difference does it make where people work or what they *do*. What we did was what we did—screwed up each other's lives. Well, I *told* you I just wanted to try it once for the experience, didn't I? I suppose it wouldn't do any good now to say I cared about you . . . still do. You always ate so much unhealthy garbage.

The dog started to whine again, scratching on the back door, and you immediately jumped from where you were sitting (on the toilet) and bumped your head on a hanging fern. I said, "Hey, wait, tell me about the yogurt factory!"

You stopped in the doorway, but didn't turn around (too bad, because I'd made a funny white wig out of the bubble bath, George Washington style).

You said, "What do you care what I eat?"

"Let's not fight. I just got here. Leave the damn dog alone for a minute."

"He's crying."

"You want *me* to cry?" I said. "Is that what would've stopped you from kicking me out?"

"Don't you have any feelings at all?"

"Whadda ya think I'm talking about? Why'd you hafta go and get a dog, anyway?"

You said, "I haven't made love with anyone since you," crying already, and you went to get the little beast.

Actually, I think I remember you'd wanted to get a cat or hamster or turtle or something so you could name it Gabriel. You'd already picked the name. That was when we first met, wasn't it? But I told you I didn't want any rug rats or linoleum lizards—I thought it was a pretty funny thing to say. You got mad and pouted for almost a week. Am I getting things mixed up? Maybe we were talking about babies. Oh, sorry—

Anyway, I don't remember how long our reunion was, maybe a week or several days or half a month. Every day you left me alone in the house with that dog, but made us stay in different rooms. You made me promise I'd leave it alone. "I know your promise isn't worth much," you said.

"You wait and see," I said, "I won't go near it," but you closed it in your bedroom anyway, protecting the cowardly little creature from me. But it bit me one day while you were at work—I'll bet you didn't know that. At least it could've bit me. It had its chance. Never mind, I'm changing some of the details, like that, because if I told you it bit me, instead of giving me another bubble bath or taking me to the hospital, you would've said, "I knew you couldn't manage to keep your promise." But I did! The stupid animal wouldn't *let* me come near him, even when I cornered him he'd scoot away between my legs.

I wish I could tell you what it was like staying in the house all day with that dog. I'd hoped for more of a reunion atmosphere, you know? Actually, I didn't spend very much time chasing him because I hardly ever saw him. He had some great hiding places. You probably know where they were because you disappeared after your lousy supper every night too. I knew you were somewhere in your bedroom. You gave me some sheets on the couch and locked all the doors before you went to bed—maybe so I couldn't sneak away at night—and all the locks needed a key, on the inside as well as the outside. That was a new touch. I wasn't going to leave anyway, I had nowhere else to go, no one was expecting me. But, just to be sure, you never gave me my clothes back after that first bubble bath. I got used to it. I wasn't cold or anything. But you should've realized I wasn't going to go anywhere that day you found me sunbathing in the front yard. I'd squeezed through a window. We used to practice that when we had fire drills, remember? It was your idea. Anyway, you jumped out of your car before turning the engine off or setting the break. (It coasted into the garden and got caught on some bushes that hadn't been trimmed in three years, I'd guess.) You covered me with your coat, twisted my arm behind my back and marched me inside. Then the lecture. No, instead of a lecture you just stood there, looking at the floor, your lashes wet and smudged. But when I went to comfort you, you socked me in the stomach. The dog was yapping in the bedroom. I was doubled up on hands and knees, trying to get my breath back, so you stepped over me and went to let the dog out. When you came back you took your coat and hung it up. I'd forgotten you used to work out in a gym. Shadow boxing? You started nailing all the windows shut and fastened boards across the doorways, like a condemned house. After that, you came in and out through the dog door, which opened into an enclosed kennel in the back yard, with a locked gate, so if I wanted to sunbathe, I had to do it there, amid all the dogshit. The only time the creature was out in the kennel was when he was shitting.

"Are you trying to punish me?" I asked.

"You're free to leave any old time you want," you said, the same thing you'd always said. You were filing your nails, as usual, looking down at your hands, blowing the dust away. You had the same little tools—gold in a neat leather case.

"You must carry that thing around in self-defense," I said.

"*You* could use one—instead of biting your nails down to the bone."

"How is occasional biting worse than obsessive filing?"

"It's ugly and gross."

"I suppose fido uses a manicure kit."

You filed vigorously. "He's clean and he's not promiscuous."

"Okay, I knew you'd have to bring it up eventually," I said. "It's not as though I was keeping dark secrets."

"Not much!"

"I was trying to spare your feelings."

"What a crock! You still think I'm an idiot?" You must've been filing away the end of your finger by then. "You still think I never took a sex-education class?"

"It was a joke," I said. "I didn't know you'd believe me."

"Stop talking about it. I don't want to hear about it or think about it." You threw the gold nail file at me. It stuck into the carpet like a knife, so I picked it up and held it on my chest, pretending it was stabbed into my heart and I was dying. Then you threw a pillow at me. "Is everything always a joke to you?"

"No, I'm dead serious."

"Stop it!" The windows rattled. Then you whined, "How could you do that to me. You never even told me *why*."

"I missed it."

"*I* was satisfied."

"I missed *it*."

"Selfish brat." You got off the sofa, snatched the nail file from me, then sat again and started filing your already perfect toenails.

"I offered to share."

"That's sick."

"You got a boy dog, didn't you?" I said. Maybe you didn't notice I was smiling. "Wimpy, yes, but a boy."

"You're really sick!" You must've thrown the nail file at me again, but I didn't notice until it hit me. It scratched my cheek a little. You were trying to shout at me but your voice was quivering. "You never really wanted me—you're admitting it. Why can't you just stay away from me?" Then you threw the whole leather case at me, and all the gold tools flew out of it, so I ducked.

"I don't know," I said.

When I uncovered my head, you were gone. You were right, in a way. I don't mean about being sick. But I don't know why I decided, in spite of everything, I would try to make us want each other again.

I guess I want to tell you what I did all day while you were at work. You never gave me a chance to explain. But I can't remember. It was nice to have nothing to do for a change, but I can't imagine spending all day doing nothing. I picked dog hairs out of the sofa. The scrawny pooch never even cried and scratched on the inside of your bedroom door. You were gone eight or nine hours every day and I had to pee at least four times before you came home. How'd the dog manage to hold it? Probably went blue in the face. That's probably the only reason he seemed so wild to see you when you came home. You always threw your coat and sales brochures on the floor and headed straight for your room. By the time you came out with the dog (letting it hide its head under your arm, so it wouldn't have to see me while you were whisking it outside), I'd already hung your coat up and stacked the brochures on the coffee table. But you went back to the coat and got out a different hanger and hung it up yourself.

I gave you a few days to cool down. I found a bathrobe in the hall closet and wore it most of the time, even though it was too long and swished around on the floor, picking up dust and dog fuzz; almost tripping me. You weren't paying attention. I could've been dressed like a Fourth Avenue hooker, and you'd've never batted an eye. I know you don't go for that kind of stuff.

I did finally come up with a plan, which I shouldn't have to tell you because I know you noticed. (Although I wonder if you noticed that I'd even shaved—it wasn't until after I'd finished that I remembered you preferred everything hairy.)

I let you take care of the dog, waiting for you to come back into the living room. "Hey, sweetheart," I said.

"Don't give me that bull. What've you been doing all day? Butter wouldn't melt in your mouth."

"Butter causes hardening of the arteries."

"I don't want to hear any more of your crap."

"Okay," I said. "I won't say another word." I went into the bathroom and wrapped about ten towels around me, then turned on the radio. The classical station was playing harp music—that was no good. I couldn't find the jazz station. I should've investigated a good music station before you came home, but there wasn't time, I guess. I don't remember why I didn't. Part of the day I was trying to pick the lock you'd put on your bedroom door, but I didn't want to tell you that. (I'd only been trying to see if you still grew plants all over your room. I'd forgotten to notice before while chasing fido out from under the bed.) I finally found a teen station playing something bouncy. Then I started to dance!

Don't tell me you didn't watch because you sat there on the sofa with a glass of cheap wine and the newspaper in your lap, but you never turned a page. After I'd removed about four of the towels, your eyes were glowing, hot and bright, like silver foil embers in a phony fire. I had you. I almost had you. I probably flipped the next three towels away too quickly, but I could move easier after that, and the bouncy song switched to a slow romantic grind. Perfect. You always liked that kind of stuff. And I was great. I'd never done better even when I was a professional dancer. Boy, don't tell me you weren't impressed! The wine ran down your chin and dribbled onto the newspaper, right on the comics, maybe Marmaduke or Snoopy. "Hey, get the damn dog in here now," I said. (I forgot I wasn't supposed to say anything. Maybe that was my big mistake.) I was a little out of breath—a little out of shape since I couldn't ride my bike anymore. "Get the dog in here *now* and see what it does," I said. "You gotta make it face things. Why can't you do that?"

"You don't know anything about sensitive dogs," you said. Your voice was flat. Your eyes almost rotating inside their sockets. Burning holes into me—we were that close. "They're scared of everything." You finished the wine, but missed your mouth with half of it. The front of your shirt was wet. "They trust everything. I mean, they don't trust *any*thing anymore." The newspaper sort of floated to the floor. You were standing. I stopped dancing, the last towel gone, and we were eye-to-eye, breathing in each other's faces. Yours was a warm wine smell. *Both* of us were panting—don't tell me you weren't. There was an explosion of air between us each time we exhaled. Oh God, we were close, so *close* . . . then none of that old crap would've mattered anymore.

"I mean, they trust everything *once,*" you said.

"Then what? Die?"

"You don't know anything. You never did. Always an easy joke . . . or an easy lie."

"It wasn't easy for me either. You think it was easy? It wasn't. I was scared."

You said, "I don't want to talk about it."

"You *never* want to talk about it!"

You tried to whip me with one of the towels and yelled, "I don't even want to think about it!" The towel didn't make much of an impression. You headed for your room.

"Why'd you go and get a dog?" I shouted. "You know what that dog does all day? Hides under your bed. *Hides!* From what? It's alone in your goddamn garden of Eden, but it hides!"

"You don't know anything."

"I know the damn dog *hides* all day!"

"What do *you* know about dogs," you said. "That dog loves me, can't you tell? *He* won't come home pregnant and tell me it's a miracle of our love, then laugh behind my back. I know you were laughing, don't tell me you weren't!"

"So let it in right now and see how much it loves you. *Boom,* right under the sofa."

"Because of *you.*"

"Then why doncha admit to it that *you* invited me here," I said. "It was all your idea. Hey, pooch, if I'm scaring you to death, blame your housemate here, it's not *my* fault. Why do *I* always get all the blame? We were supposed to have a simple little reunion." I grabbed something—I don't remember what, the wine bottle or a lamp—and rushed at you, but you slammed your door in my face. I was as strong as you and you knew it. "Hey!" I kicked the door.

"You don't know anything about sensitive dogs." Your voice came from behind the door, muffled, as though you were face down on your bed. "You stay away from that dog. He'll stay loyal even if he's scared to death."

"Don't try to make it sound like that dog is victimized all day."

"How do I know it isn't?"

"Damn you—you're always so quick to blame me. Why don't I just leave right now—leave and never come back? How would that be?" I kicked the door again, but you didn't answer. "Hey! Are you crying?"

"Shut up."

"If that was *my* dog, I'll tell you who'd be the one who was hurt. It would tear me up—it living under sofas and beds, scrambling from one to the other, always trembling and crouching like I was going to clobber it." I dropped the wine bottle and went back to the sofa, lay down face first, so you probably couldn't hear me anymore, with my face against the cushion, but, in case you're interested, I said, "It probably wouldn't even take a piece of meat from my hands. It would starve first. How's *that* supposed to make me feel?"

When I rolled over, you were standing there staring at me. Then you turned away, without a word, and went to fix the dog's supper. I lay there on the couch. There was no place for you to sit, but you didn't seem to mind. You straightened up the room, turned the radio off, threw the wine bottle away, watered all the plants (that took almost half an hour), then sat on the rug, in a corner, under the biggest potted tree, crossed your legs, folded your hands and looked at me, but without the silver foil embers. The room got darker and darker. Pretty soon I couldn't see your eyes anymore. But I guess you were still sitting there, your eyes like the water at the bottom of a well, which you can't see unless you jump in and hit it.

I didn't say anything until you got up. But I forget what I said. Maybe you remember. Something stupid like "Hey, honey." I know I should've said I'm sorry. But, believe me, I hadn't ever laughed at you. I had been sorry the whole time. It was such a crazy excuse, I'd known it as soon as the words came out, but I couldn't think of anything else. I didn't know you'd go around the house singing for two straight days.

You didn't answer.

"Where're you going?" I asked.

"To get Pepper."

"Pepper? That's his name? What happened to Gabriel?"

You were already outside. You had to unlock the kennel door to get the dog because it wouldn't come back through the pet door. Not with me sitting there. But then you didn't head for the bedroom right away.

"Where're you going now?"

"Pepper's not used to being outside so long. He stepped in some poop." You closed the bathroom door and the water started running. Damn dog. The sound made me have to pee. I held it for a while, but the pressure was too much. I tapped on the bathroom door with just my fingertips. "Hey . . . honey?" No answer. Steam was coming from under the door. The water was still running, but it was the shower . . . at least you weren't giving the dog a bubble bath. He might've been scared of the bubbles. Then I could hear you saying, "Hold still, Pepper, hold still." Maybe you didn't know I heard you. Your voice was musical and happy. The steam smelled sweet, like strawberries and soap and the smell of your skin—whether you were sweating or freshly dressed or just woke up in the morning. My heart stopped beating and sort of felt like some big chunk of something I'd swallowed three years ago and still wouldn't go down. "Please, honey. . . ." I tapped on the door and rattled the knob. "Let me explain. Maybe I can make you feel better." I was cold. That was the first time I wished I had some clothes. "It was a false alarm anyway. He'd had a vasectomy. I'd forgotten."

"Stop!" At first I thought you were still talking to the dog. But you said, "It's okay, Pepper," in a happy voice, then shouted again, "Shut up! I said shut up! I'm not going to listen anymore. Besides, that's hardly the point."

"Why?" I said. "Didn't you have the dog neutered when you got him?"

Something heavy fell, and the dog yipped, and you shrieked, "Shut up, I hate you, get out, right now!"

I don't know what happened. I was still holding the doorknob. You'll probably swear you locked it, maybe you even told the police you did, but I never bashed in that door, honey. It sort of blew open in front of me. It sort of melted open. And the wall of steam hit me. A moment of bliss. That's all. Then you were shouting again, "Hey, what the hell—get out! *I said get out!*" Before either of us could move, the dog jumped out of the shower, onto the toilet seat, onto the sink counter, slipping and scrambling, kicking plants and stuff all over the floor. A jar filled with guest soap exploded when it hit the edge of the tub. Sounded like a scream. "Get out, get out, get out!" You were wet like a seal and slipping in the tub, but you couldn't go anywhere because I was in the way. The damn dog couldn't find the door. You finally pushed me aside, right into the broken glass. "Hide somewhere, so he'll calm down." You jumped from the tub to the sink counter to the toilet to the clothes hamper, chasing the dog, calling, "Here, Pepper, come on, don't be afraid," your voice sweet and low, then turning to me to scream, "Hide, get out of sight, he hates you, he'll kill himself to get away from you."

"Where should I go?"

"Anywhere! Anywhere that's out of sight, just go!"

Didn't you know you and the dog were between me and the door? I was dancing on all that broken glass. So I jumped into the linen closet and folded myself onto a shelf, my head between my knees, a close-up view of the blood oozing out of my feet and onto what I recognized as your best cream-colored towels. I'd never cried into them before. What a mess we'd made. I guess the dog finally found the door, and you followed. Everything got very quiet. Just the shower spattering. I balled up one of the towels and pressed it to my face and breathed the towel smell for a while. Then I rolled over and was about to slide off the shelf—I was on my stomach, one leg dangling to the floor, towels jumbled all around me—and I saw you in the doorway. You were standing there, still holding the dog. The beast looked exhausted, as though it had stopped caring. You were sobbing into his already soaked and matted fur. There was a bite on your cheek, a trickle of blood which you kept licking with your tongue. But the dog was dead. I could tell. Its neck was broken.

I lay there on the shelf, biting the towel, until you looked up. I don't know if you noticed the blood and glass and dirt from the plants all over the floor, the closet full of bloody towels, the shower still running, the steam which didn't smell very sweet anymore. I said, "Honey, sweetheart. . . ."

"No, go away."

"Please. . . ."

"It's not safe for you here, can't you see that?"

But when was it ever, honey, think about that. When was it safe for anyone?

The Dove Hunters

Sometimes when a dove is hit, it may sit on the ground like a nesting chicken and not appear wounded at all.

Ronnie is the bird dog. She keeps her eye on the doves as they fall, staring at the spot where she sees them land. Then Bill waits on the trail while Ronnie follows her eye and finds the bird, usually not yet dead. He taught her to do this: she holds the body with one hand, thumb and forefinger of the other hand in a ring around the bird's neck, jerks her hands apart, pops the head off, drains blood from the limp neck. As Bill's vest fills with birds, its heavy bottom is dark and wet with still more blood that drains slowly after the hearts stop beating.

Her name is Sophronia, which he shortened to Ronnie.

They leave at 3 a.m. to drive two hours into the back country, wearing boots and jeans, long-sleeved shirts and canvas vests on a September morning which will be close to 90 degrees by 11. At dawn and before, the doves will feed in the stubble fields and drink from square pools that were once water holes for cattle. The way they used to hunt was for Bill to find a rain wash or gully where they could keep hidden and wait near one of the pools for the doves to come in; and they used to share the gun. Sitting together in a gully—facing opposite directions, side-by-side, shoulders touching—if the one without the gun saw a bird, by the time the gun was passed, the bird was out of range. A few times when Ronnie spotted one, Bill just turned and shot it himself; then Ronnie stopped watching for birds and stretched out in the gully, pretending to sleep. So Bill said she could have the gun to herself for a half hour later. Once as she sat waiting, Ronnie started picking at the sediments in the steep side of the gully. The hard dirt broke away in pieces. Ronnie removed a long section of earth, like a brick, and saw part of a small snake, not its head or tail, somewhere in the middle. She nudged Bill and showed him, then replaced the piece of dirt.

The method they use now is to keep moving. There is a thin rabbit trail, barely discernible through the fields, but Bill always knows where it is and stays on it. Bill walks in front, Ronnie follows the blood-soaked vest. Bill carries the gun under one arm, muzzle to the ground. Once Bill spoke of getting Ronnie her own gun.

"Watch out for snakes, Ronnie."

"I'm watching."

The snakes won't be out until the sun is.

"You wouldn't waste a shot on a snake, would you," she says.

"Of course not!"

"Yes, I remember how disgusted you were when

you told me about Dottie trying to run over a snake on purpose."

"Yeah, she swerved way into the other lane."

"And you were pulling on the wheel to keep her from hitting it."

"Yes."

"Were you mad—screaming at her?"

"Yes. I know I was mad, I'm not sure if I screamed."

"You screamed at her a lot, though."

"Yes."

"What for—what types of things would make you yell at her?"

"You've already heard all about it."

"I couldn't have heard *every*thing."

"Everything I care to remember."

"Come on!"

He can't hear Ronnie's footsteps because she walks with the same rhythm that he does. He hears her breathing. The dawn looks like dusk but has a different smell. There's no dew on the high desert. Doves are the only birds around here that don't ever glide, and their wings whistle when they take off. They're swift fliers and the shot has to be made well ahead of the flight path so pellets and bird will arrive at the same place at the same time. Bill picks up his used shells to reload them at home.

She talks to his back and the vest and the growing spot of blood. "You screamed at her for everything except what you should've screamed at her for."

"I was screaming at her before I even knew about that."

"But when you found out, you didn't even yell about it."

"There was no point."

"Maybe not," she says. "I would've yelled anyway."

Unlike vultures, doves do not choose one mate for life and are seldom at peace with each other. They'll literally pick each other apart.

"You told me you used to feel relieved when she would leave for work in the morning," she says. "Didn't you stop and think about what that meant?"

"I didn't want to know what it meant."

"I used to have this roommate I hated," she says. "When I heard her car pull in I would say 'oh shit.' Did you say that when Dottie came home?"

"Not in those words."

"What would you do when she came home?"

"I've told you all this stuff about a thousand times."

"You mean: she would bitch about having to work and about you not doing the dishes because you studied all day, and then she would take a nap, then you'd both go jogging and you noticed how fat her ass was."

"All of that didn't happen over and over every day."

"But that was about it, wasn't it?"

"I guess."

"Maybe you didn't yell at her when you found out what she was doing because you were glad—because it meant you could leave her. Were you glad?"

"I'm glad *now.*"

"What did you feel *then*?"

"For Chrissake, Ronnie, I don't remember!"

"You were hurt."

"Okay, I was hurt, now can't we drop this subject for the hundredth time?"

A cottontail breaks from cover and runs ahead of them up the trail. Bill aims the gun but doesn't fire. He can feel Ronnie's breath on the back of his neck. "Sorry, honey, I wasn't fast enough."

Ronnie loves rabbit stew. Once she suggested he could wait in a gully while she flushed out the rabbits and made them run *toward* him. He shook his head. "I've never tried it that way."

"Then let's do it!" she said.

"No, you might get hurt."

She just smiled a little and looked away.

"Was there a reason she fooled around?" she asks.

"I don't know. She never told me."

"Didn't you tell me that she said something about your sex life to the marriage counselor?"

"I guess so."

"Like she didn't get enough?"

"It wasn't that. You know what she said."

"That *he* was more fun."

Bill nudges a stone off the trail with the toe of his boot.

"How often did you do it with her?" she asks.

"I didn't keep score. Probably two or three times a week."

"Oh."

Although still on the path, they have to push through tumbleweeds, sage and wild oats that grow on either side of the trail and lean across it. The eastern sky is light now but the sun hasn't cleared the hills. They'll get to the end of the trail, near a sandy wash, at sunrise. They hunt every weekend during the season.

While walking beside one of the deepest rain washes, Bill points with the gun so Ronnie will notice the jack rabbit standing behind a bush, staring at them.

"Didn't you notice her fat ass and flabby legs while you were doing it?" she asks.

"I don't think so."

"And then she had the audacity to say you weren't any good—even though you were nice enough not to mention her big ass."

"Things aren't that simple."

"At least I was positive and helpful."

"Yes you were." He lifts the gun and aims, circling slowly, but there are no birds in sight.

"You're not worrying too much about what I said, are you?"

"I guess not."

"That's good." She puts a hand on the back of his neck; he jumps a little. "How did you do it with her—the same way?"

"I think so." Bill shifts the gun to his other arm and stops to wipe his brow. Then he turns and faces Ronnie but is still sweating.

"Why don't you remember?" she asks.

"Christ, Ronnie, I've laid it all out over and over—what the hell are you still looking for?"

"I'm not sure anymore."

The path weaves in and out among the square pools of water. Since he always picks up his spent cartridges, there's no sign that they've been on this same trail every weekend.

He stops. "This is where I got two in one shot last week. It sure had been a long time since I'd done that!"

Ronnie stares off to the side. Quail are calling in the underbrush.

"You're not tired, are you, Ronnie?" Bill asks.

She shakes her head. They both turn westward and stand motionless to catch one of the infrequent morning breezes.

"As usual, not enough of it," he says, turning to face her again. Then he smiles. "Well, if you get tired of this, we don't have to go all the way. We can go on home now."

"You mean if I get bored we'll quit rather than try a different way."

"I can't think of any other effective way to hunt."

"No, I don't suppose you can."

After a moment, they begin walking again, still single file. Bill misses on his next several shots. The birds fly to the east, but circle around in front toward the next water hole.

"Fat ass, flabby legs, whiney voice, bitchy complainer, messed around—how could you stand living with her?" she asks.

"I don't know."

"I mean, did you actually *want* to screw her?"

Bill stops, stands aside, looks quickly at Ronnie, then points with the gun to some deer droppings on the trail in front of his boots. But he lifts the gun quickly as a dove comes into range, moving left to right in front of them. He shoots twice. Ronnie leaves the trail to get the fallen bird, then comes back, dropping the head out in the bushes for scavengers.

"You must've been desperately horny when you were younger."

The meadowlarks are singing, bravely flying

about—its against the law to shoot them, likewise hawks and owls. Ronnie's pace has slowed and she is dragging her boots in the dust. He glances back. She's no longer scanning the fields for doves that are landing or taking off.

"Did you ever try anything different with her?" she asks.

"A couple of times which I've already told you about."

"And one of them was good, wasn't it." She sounds far away.

He stops but does not look back. "So okay, I had *a* good time. Satisfied?"

"No." She drags her feet more heavily until she finally catches up to him.

"Well, it's not as though I keep talking about her or comparing you to her—*you're* the one who can't seem to forget it."

"I've seen pictures of the two of you. You were happy."

"Ronnie—why do you do this to yourself! Would it make you feel better if I said I hated her and I knew I hated her every second of every day, and I hated her most of all when I fucked her?"

"No."

"What the hell do you want!" He resumes walking.

After several steps, Ronnie almost bumps into Bill's back because he's standing still on the trail again. He points out a small hawk sitting in a dead tree, but she isn't looking, so he nudges her and points again.

"So you liked whatever it was you tried with her," she says.

"It was okay."

"That's all?"

He turns and looks at her. "It wasn't good enough for *her*. Is that what you want to hear?"

The last time Ronnie had used the gun, she shot a hawk. It was a small one, flying swiftly, so she had mistaken it for a dove. Bill had to bury it and make sure no feathers remained, and he hadn't slept well that night, even though no one could've possibly seen them.

"Bill . . . do you feel like it *now*?"

Bill scans the horizon for incoming doves. He can hear the frantic whistle of wings, but sees nothing. The sky is growing much lighter. He shifts the weight of the vest on his back. *"Now?"*

"Yes!"

The stiff canvas vest creaks a little, like a saddle, when he shifts his weight and transfers the gun to his left arm, looks around, passes the gun back to his right arm. "I know you want something different, but . . . in the weeds? On the ground and rocks? In hunting clothes?"

She looks down at her boots. There are a few drops of blood in the dust on her right toe from the last dove she drained. A flock of five birds suddenly take off a few hundred feet ahead and circle, wings whistling. Bill turns and watches them all the way around, until the doves land near the same spot they had been before.

Then she says, "Could I have the gun a while? I haven't shot for a long time."

Bill looks down at the gun which he didn't lift and aim when the doves circled them. "No." He looks up grinning. "It's been too long. You might miss and shoot *me*!"

His grin fades before she answers it with one of her own. "It would look like a hunting accident, wouldn't it."

They can hear the grasses rustle before the next breeze hits them. They both turn to face it, lifting their arms away from their sides, closing their eyes.

The sun is up and already glaring and already hot. Flies begin buzzing, searching for the heads of doves left in the underbrush, already rotting.

The trail has become sandy and their boots pad in it softly.

Shut Up

The dog knows from habit to chase the screaming ambulance. On her way home from reading tarot cards in a vegetarian restaurant, Frances eagerly follows her collie who loves the sound of his own voice.

The first time a big paramedic van had whipped past them on this same block, she'd had to drag the protesting, howling dog all the way to the accident. Once there, he forgot the pain in his ears, even forgot to bark at the variety of strange men, any one of whom might someday follow Frances home from the cafe. Frances knew, once she made Lucky accompany her to where an ambulance had stopped, he'd follow willingly after that, might even take the lead. "Dogs turn into their primal selves at the sight and smell of pain," she often told someone else at a site. "They love it, search for it; they'll lick someone else's wounds as eagerly as they do their own." Lucky licks his wounds while Frances has to amuse herself in other ways, finding some small diversion in the faces of the cafe guests who stare at her fearless uniqueness. She wears a cowboy hat, her long gray-streaked hair in braids, an Indian fringed dress, and boots—either mountaineer or cowboy, depending on the need. The cards, of course, are a crock. But she also finds some entertainment in the men she leads home—after flipping an effective card—wondering vaguely afterwards why it didn't seem to be what she'd hoped for. The dog waits outside the bedroom door, barking, urging them to finish and leave quickly. The bark is rough and the sex rougher.

The ambulance lights up the whole street corner, blinking red and white, glittering red-and-white in puddles and across the rainbows in oil slicks. They already have the stretcher unfolded, positioned next to the door of a sedan which has its hood wrinkled into a telephone pole, two wheels up on the sidewalk. Lucky lifts his nose, eyes shut, sniffing, almost tasting, then drooling over the sight and aroma of the driver of the green sedan who is seated on the stretcher, feet on the ground, head in his hands, blood on his knuckles.

Most of the other people are on the corner sidewalk, near the end of the ambulance, and on the other side of the street, watching the scene like a movie without close-ups. "Go home," a paramedic shouts.

"Vultures," Frances agrees with him. He glares over his glasses. "Yes, vultures," she continues. "They hover at a distance and wait for death, wait for it to finish." The man on the stretcher looks up at her too, over his hands.

"Go home, Frances," the paramedic says.

"No, I'm not like them. I'm not looking for *that.* I've heard steam will rise from a living wound. *You* know what's important here, you've seen it: how people *don't* die, not how they do."

The paramedic shakes his head. "You really believe those weird cards, huh, Frances?"

"They're bullshit."

She follows the white plume at the tip of Lucky's tail into the alley where there are no street lamps. Behind the storefronts, six cottages were built during the war. Frances moved in when she was twenty, right after V-J Day. She'd always had a dog, but never married. She takes birth-control pills—has since they came on the market, and just can't remember to stop now that the danger has faded. She'd aborted original teenaged ideas of having kids, abhors the idea of them clinging to her legs, their fuzzy heads just reaching her crotch. She'd always done most of what she does now—in the daytime she makes ugly clay statues for tasteless people while the dog sleeps, his chin on her ankle, barks only when someone approaches, and only if it's a man.

Lucky goes on into the cottage, but Frances stops outside to feel her kiln, to see if the night air has cooled it enough. She can load more ugly statues into it tomorrow. Across the court, her neighbor's bedroom light is still on—the window glass is milky, but he has no curtains, and she sees the blond glow of his hair and profile. She watches him come and go, his eyes seem soft; and if he didn't have sideburns, she would wonder if he was old enough to shave or have girls. Yet he is man enough to make Lucky bark, and he might be the one who complained recently. That's why the landlord said she might have to get rid of the dog. She thinks she probably loves Lucky, although how can she tell?

Her hands are smeared, coated with clay. He comes across the court with a plastic cup, raps gently on the screen door. He knows her name: "Frances, could I borrow a cup of vinegar?"

She kneels, unzips his pants, takes him out and blows him, backing him up until he shatters with his back against the wall. Faintly she can taste the clay fingerprints she left on him like stains before using her mouth to clean him.

He looks at her with drowsy brown eyes, his torso flattened, leaning near the door, his knees bent, holding himself there until he says, "Thanks," without a smile.

He goes home to sing.

She knows Morgan sings. He told her when he moved in that he has to practice. Perhaps this is just the first time she's ever really heard him, although he may have been mood music in the background during anything she's done. She may've humped someone to the sound of his voice: sweet, like warm caramel. Frances holds her cheeks, one in each palm, then hugs herself, then holds her heaving breast and never pauses to wonder if this is mind expanding or relevant. She has to kneel, to sink and sit back on her feet, her heels grind in and she rocks on them, and his molasses voice is as exciting to her ears as Lucky's tongue (she pushes the dog away now), as smooth to her ears as his cock was to her mouth. She remembers he is silky, pungently basic smelling, like clay. He breathes for a crescendo, pours every possible drop of air into the song's climax, and she digs her fists between her knees, presses down the dress material which stretches across her thighs, forces all her weight onto the heel she's sitting on, and nearly finishes as the song ends, but not quite. She shudders and suddenly she is rigid and old and her breath short, and the foot she's sitting on is asleep, numb, and the song is over, finished without agony. She knows somehow pleasure and pain are the same, doesn't know what this boy has to do with her cruelly painless nights.

Her dog bites him.

He comes out of his cottage with a girl who's wearing only shorts and a bikini top. They carry towels. And Morgan is also wearing shorts. His legs pale and thin, Frances recognizes the bulge at his crotch. She's at the wheel cupping slimy hands around an urn, one of two thousand. Morgan puts the girl in his car—really a lovely girl, looks like Lucky, long tricolor hair and a loud voice. He says, "Just a sec," and comes back toward the house, running slightly, leaps for his doorstep. Lucky leaps also, bites his tempting thigh.

The wound turns purple and red. Frances kneels before familiar knees to dab pine-tar medicine on the teeth marks. His whole thigh turns black and greasy until she can't tell the difference between the pine tar and the slippery clay from her hands. She keeps patting the wound with one hand, the other hand moves directly to his zipper, frees him and coats him with clay, then pulls him into her mouth, holds his legs with both hands, one behind each knee. She pauses to say, "The dog's just jealous. I don't understand it myself—jealousy—we have a perfectly open marriage." She sucks thoughtfully, then says, "Times like this I remember the dog I had as a girl on my father's farm. When time came to slaughter the rabbits we raised, I had to tie him. See, my father fastened the rabbits up by their hind legs then killed them quickly with a hammer behind their ears. The dog never cared about a dead rabbit, the steaming guts in the bucket, the blood kicked out after the head was gone, didn't even care about the dressed meat and didn't seem to notice the fatty stink of death. But if my father didn't hit it right, the rabbit screamed—like a girl . . . no, like nothing you've heard. A deathcry. Imagine the voice of a sweet white bunny, and that would be it, a deathcry. Well, the dog would go crazy if the rabbit screamed—panting, drooling, trying to get over there and bite it. I don't know why." It's hard to talk with her mouth full of him. Probably hard to understand too. She gathers her saliva and swallows, empties her mouth to say, "I'm sorry he bit you, but it's important that it hurts. If you don't feel pain, you're dead. If you do feel it—"

He tucks himself away. "That's pretty cheap, Frances," he says. "I don't have time. You're always trying to do this and I don't have time whenever the whim strikes you."

She sits back on her heels. He can't even say rough words roughly. "Morgan, wait, I wanted to tell you *why* Lucky's sorry for this—the manager says he bothers everyone, and if I don't want to move or lose him, I'll have to have his voice removed."

Morgan is already at his car. She bites her lower lip and is grateful at least for the salty taste as her teeth grip and grind the lip like gristle. But when she opens her mouth to free the lip, once again her feet are falling asleep, one knee itches where some pebbles are embedded, her back aches, her stomach growls. All mere annoyances, nothing which drastically stands out.

She is still at the wheel, on the two-thousandth pot, when Morgan returns, red and streaked and salty, still accompanied by the girl with tricolor hair. He puts her into the house, sucking on her mouth at the door, their lips cross the threshold. Then the door closes, and inside a shower begins, and Morgan does not limp as he approaches Frances, his leg washed clean, the bite is blue and green, the crotch of his shorts relaxed.

"I'm finished, Morgan," she says. "Let me go in and get this stuff off my hands first."

"Not first, Frances. Last. The last was this afternoon."

"Come on—you never got that cup of vinegar."

"Frances—"

She is already inside the house, shutting the dog in the bedroom. Morgan stops just inside the door.

"Frances—"

She sits on her heels, arranging her patchwork-quilt skirt around her in a circle. She's wearing jeans beneath it. She settles heavily. She hasn't washed her hands after all.

"Sing for me—give me a concert, okay?"

"No."

She lunges, stumps across the floor on her knees, clutches his hips.

"Watch it—I'm sunburned."

"I won't scorch my tongue."

"No, you sure won't!" But he is probably afraid to jerk himself away from her: she's holding onto him through his shorts.

"We aren't going to do this anymore, Frances."

"But we're *doing* it." Now she has him out, hanging like a tongue. "How'd you get sandy *here*?"

"Frances—" He tries to take it back, but she squeezes the base and he's got to be afraid. He holds onto her shoulders to keep himself from falling backwards and ripping it out of her mouth or tearing it off altogether.

"Where's your spine, boy, you're like a noodle."

"I'm obviously not interested."

"Sing!"

"No."

Frances looks up, raises her eyebrows and rolls her eyes to the top of her head. She pulls back her lips and holds on with her teeth. "Remember about pain, Morgan," she says thickly, then releases and backs away.

Lucky is hoarse like an old man, and Frances asks the vet if she can keep his vocal cords in a jar of formaldehyde. "I didn't cut them *out*," he says. "Just slit them so they're not functional." So she makes two large marbles of soft clay and drops them in a jelly jar of alcohol, carries it carefully—and Lucky follows silently—to the cafe to read cards. Lucky has a place—a silk, fringed pillow, stained dark from unnoticeable dirt he carries. He never used to bark inside the cafe anyway. Tonight the guests all want him to try, as Frances moves from table to table, offering to read cards, showing the jar. They turn to the dog and say, "Make him bark, make him try." And occasionally Lucky lifts his head and looks back with dull animal eyes, licks his mouth, sighs and tries to swallow the lump in his throat.

Frances still waits—this night like all others—for Morgan to visit the cafe, to slip through the hanging bead curtain, like swimming, like the way his smooth body would part water, the way she'd parted her lips for him. Other men still follow her home—now Lucky will no longer bark at the bedroom door. She sacrificed the rough voice in order to keep her bed in the same damp wood-walled bedroom, in order to at least *see* Morgan daily and rub her tongue hard against her teeth when he walks past or when she hears his voice as he talks on the telephone. So she waits—each night better than the last, better that he never comes here, anticipation mounting all evening at the cafe with his agonizing absence. It's almost painful *enough.* And he no longer sings—unless he does his singing at home while she's here. Her flesh twitches at the thought—not that he sings somewhere, but because he doesn't sing *here:* wherever she is at any time is where he never sings, not anymore. So she waits, the aching silence of his singing is as arousing as the voice itself, makes her wait, makes her shudder and wait, makes her bite her hand and wait.

The manager of the group of cottages is hypnotized by her potter's wheel.

"Notice," she says, also not removing her eyes from the lump of clay which leans from side to side between her hands, "notice that my dog isn't barking at you."

"Where is he?" The man's eyes seem to rotate inside his head in unison with the wheel.

"There." She nods toward the house. Lucky comes to the door, stands behind the screen, licks his lips, smacking softly as though trying to taste something. He looks down, ashamed. A wasted gesture, however, as the manager won't even turn to see him. "I had his voice removed, see?" Frances lifts the jar she keeps on the ground next to her ankle.

"Ah, Frances. . . ." He actually reaches out to touch the wheel.

"No-ya-don't." She slaps his hand away, stops pumping and the wheel slows. She keeps her hands cupped around the clay until it completes the last twirl. "Now, what is it, honey?"

"Frances, you're going to have to move anyway. A majority of the tenants—well, I can't say more, you just have to move, that's all."

Frances stands. "I stole my dog's voice!" She plants the jar of clay vocal cords in the center of the wet lump on the wheel. "I saved these things to *prove* it." She pumps the lever with one foot, the wheel rotates, the alcohol sloshes softly. "Look—two globs saved in a jar like castrated balls."

The manager's eyes once again go around, watching the jar. "I can't help it. You and your dog will have to go. One of the tenants was *bitten*."

"By which of us?" She puts a finger in her mouth, cleans the clay from it, spits on the concrete near the pointed toe of her dusty cowboy boot, stands and takes the jar into the house. "Want something yummy for dinner, Lucky?"

She carefully dresses carelessly in a long dress from India: just two squares tied together at the sides, faded orange, casually—but effectively—wrinkled. Also corduroy pants, once brown, now nearly white, with blue denim patches on the knees which never show because the dress reaches her shins. Her belt buckle under her dress makes a lump on her stomach. Her Vietnam jungle boots are not as heavy as her other boots. She takes her pill and performs a breast examination. She wears peacock feather earrings. She thinks perhaps she burned herself while cooling the kiln—sticks her fingers in her mouth. The dog is swallowing, not rushing ahead of her to the door, as she takes the tarot cards and prepares to fascinate the evening diners.

"Come on," she says, but Lucky is still behind her when she reaches the door.

Frances hears the familiar sounds of a bedroom: burrowing, thumping, scraping, working, digging. But it's not coming from *her* bedroom—dim and blue aired behind her with one fly near the ceiling making aimless circles. Other bedrooms might sound exactly the same as hers, except now she hears a throaty laugh.

Frances is always mute in her bedroom: As soon as she would drop her skirt in a ring around her boots—leaving it there to wrinkle—she let the dog make all the sounds: sniffing the crack between the door and floor, whining, woofing, then continuing a steady rhythmic bark; and Frances would time herself—waiting for the final sad howl, pictured Lucky's slim nose pointing up, his mouth a tiny uncanine o—and she tried to finish then, but never did. Instead she just stopped. She never faked it. She wished the man would slap her for punishment instead of apologizing to her. It was *her* fault. And she never said anything nor made a sound until he left, then she sighed or hummed and stroked Lucky's belly.

Lucky doesn't want to go. Frances has to use a leash which usually stays in the closet. Lucky braces like a mule in the doorway, but Frances tugs, his collar digs in under his ears, his toenails begin to pry under the doorsill. Then he pops out of the house. His plume tail hangs limp and blends with the feathers on the backs of his legs. He follows, nose to the ground, as Frances takes a short trip from her own porch to Morgan's.

She knows what it is, what she's hearing, *knows* what it is, opens the door, brings Lucky inside, wonders if he'll bark when he smells it, then remembers: of course not. His toenails tick on the hardwood floor in the living room. The bedroom door is open. Morgan has two beds—one is standing against the walls, mattress covering one window, box spring over the other. The light from his bedroom hasn't been visible to her lately. And the room is thick with echoless padded walls, danker than her own room has ever been even though it has the same dark wood panels with black knots, the same brown rug. Finally enough light stares into the doorway with her so she can see Morgan groaning on the other bed with the horse-maned girl.

Low and rich and sweet as his singing, yet thick

like clay, like pine tar oozing from a tree, thick in her ears instead of her mouth. She bites her palm. Most of her joints sweat, mingling with the earthy smell of the bedroom. His voice in the dim room is hot, and hotly, wetly licks the insides of Frances's ears. Her stomach growls, her breath makes the sniffing sound at the doorway, her fingernails scratch the doorjamb.

The dog howls—*some*thing howls, borrowing her throat and vocal cords for the sad finale. But she isn't ready: "Not yet!" She kicks the dog across the room, braces herself spread-eagle in the bedroom doorway, her mouth and eyes sweat at the corners. She imagines clay slip on her hands, rubbing it between her fingers, wiping it off on the ass of her jeans, or on her actual ass. Like when she works ceramics naked and finishes the day dirt lined, sticky and exhausted. She opens her mouth to pant, dull eyed and hot. The girl also opens her mouth, arches her back—on top of Morgan, *on top of him*!

The room is much lighter: moonrise, sunrise, fluorescent, electric, candle light, eyesight like a cat's at night, a bonfire on the bed and Frances warms her hands, nothing to roast and put hot into her mouth, her voice like Lucky's through the crack of her bedroom door, whining, "Morgan, sing for me, I'm—"

Jealous. She wants to groan the word the same way they're groaning, or bleed it out, let the intangible pain *be* the silvery taste of a wound she always wanted to lick: her own—open, deep and sad—gnawing at her continuously over not being lucky enough to have someone torment her like this before.

"Morgan, sing, please Morgan, for me!" She flips the front of the Indian dress over her head, knocking the cowboy hat off behind her back. "Morgan, please. . . ." She unzips her pants, removes the belt from every loop, peels down the pants, stands first on one foot then the other, yanking them inside out over her feet. They won't come off over her boots. Her voice bubbles up from her throat, "*Please* Morgan, sing." He doesn't see, hasn't opened his eyes once, holds onto the girl who bounces on him, her hair flying, spreading, softly slapping her back like a horse's tail. And the wet swishing sound they are making *is* a song, and Frances is ready: spasms start from her toes, legs, knees, crotch, guts, chest, lungs. She sinks, legs melt beneath her, fists over her ears. He moans, she nearly finishes, falling forward, on knees and elbows, a finger in each ear. Nearly in agony, nearly there. So Lucky rises, drags his chain, approaches from the rear, savagely bites her leg, the goose-bumped hide of her calf, while Morgan fucks her heart and she cries like a virgin.

From Hunger

Many times he could've said, "You claim you're an artist. What kind of artist is it who never paints anything?" It came to that anyway. Whether he said it against her ear or kissed it into her mouth.

Perhaps she should've said, I could have painted you.

No. Not me. You chose the wrong subject.

Not the wrong subject, the wrong technique is all.

The only time Keith had come to Charmaine's garage-studio, he found her scraping thick wet paint off a canvas with her hands and smearing it on her face, scrubbing it in, filling her nose and ears, wiping it up and down her arms, bawling, her tears skimming over the surface of her face, sliding right off. And she put the next two fistfuls into her mouth, trying to swallow them. From behind, Keith grabbed her hair, gathering the paint-plastered strands from her face and eyes. He wound her hair in his fist, pulled her head back, punched her in the back, and she spit the mouthful up into his face.

"Breathe," he said. He slapped her spine with his palm again.

"It was lousy!" she screamed, her mouth blue and

black. She retched and blue dribbled down her chin. "It was lousy, it was such a mean bastard." She put her face against his shirt and bit a button off. She wouldn't take water to clean the paint from her throat, so he had to spit it into her mouth.

Then he supported her while she coughed against his shoulder. He still held her hair tangled in his fist. She bit his collarbone and said, "It was beautiful, so beautiful. I loved it. But it wouldn't love back." He said, "Shut up," and patted her back while she coughed on his shirt collar.

Charmaine still painted in her garage. Three huge canvases stood propped against walls, worked on so long, they'd turned black, almost by themselves. Yet all three were unfinished, practically untouched. They were a poor excuse for art—didn't make her mouth water when she faced them every morning.

Painting was in her blood: so she'd told her mother when—hungry and gaunt—she'd packed her trays and tubes, easels and canvases. She set up shop in a garage, twenty-five dollars a month with one light bulb in the ceiling and moths that stuck to the wet canvases. She painted over them every morning. She boiled the same tea bag for a week. She popped corn in a soup can over a candle, ate it with paint-smeared fingers, but she was used to the tacky taste of black, acidy red, bitter blue. Sometimes she closed her eyes, dipped her fingers into her paint tray and sucked them, trying to guess the color by the taste. She washed in a bucket. She used the garbage pails out back for a toilet—only at night, the alley had no street lamp although she could imagine her white butt like a small moon in the dark.

Week nights, Keith sold magazines door-to-door. And on weekends he played folk music with his violin in the park, his empty fiddle case at his feet, open and showing its frayed velvet lining, baited with small change, probably his laundry money. Folk tunes helped fill the case faster than sonatas or concertos could.

After college, Charmaine used to visit Keith once a week, call him or at least walk through the park and wave. But he got married, got divorced, and spent his time with the violin.

When Charmaine finished painting over moths in the morning, she and the colors (mostly black and blue) stared at each other. She hated them. Once she'd cut her finger and tried to paint with the bright blood seeping out, which had also turned black, crusty, then chipped off. Painting had yet to feed her. It had not satisfied the thumps of hungers.

If Keith wasn't playing, at least the record player would be. Charmaine didn't hear music on the other side of his door. So she knew he was still on his route. She sat in the hall with her legs straight out, bumped her head absently against his wall and tapped the toes of her sneakers together. She noticed black spots on her shoes. Her shirt was smeared with handprints. Keith came out of the elevator with a briefcase. Charmaine didn't get up or say hello. She said, "The elevator? For the second floor?"

"Hello, Charmaine."

"Getting soft?"

He unlocked his door and she followed him inside. She lay on the couch while he changed his clothes. His furniture was rented, plaid sofa and chair, two wood-grained plastic coffee tables which came unassembled—she'd helped him screw the legs in—one in front of the couch for magazines, one against the wall for the stereo and speakers. He had a few postage-stamp-sized pictures on the wall, tacked up. She noticed he'd added a few postcards, also with tacks. She thought she'd given him a few of her early paintings—maybe as a wedding gift. She didn't see them around anywhere. Maybe his wife had won them in the settlement.

The only decent room, she remembered, was the music room. The others—well, she'd never seen the bedroom, except once caught a glimpse of his unmade bed. The bathroom was too fluorescent and smelled of purple after shave. But the music room was walled on three sides with wood paneling, the fourth with the music, in alphabetical order. The center of the room was empty. She'd helped him rip the rug up in there before he was married, to help the acoustics.

"So what's up, Charmaine?" He came from the bedroom in pressed jeans and a blue sweat shirt.

"You sending the laundry out now?"

"No."

"Who's doing your ironing?" She kicked her shoes off. One landed on the coffee table, the other fell onto her stomach, so she dropped it over the side of the couch. "I'm getting expelled."

"Evicted."

"Yeah. I guess it's all over. I guess I gotta get a job

now, secretary or nurse, phone operator, teacher, waitress, housewife, mother, mistress. . . ."

He sat in the chair and crossed his legs, rested one arm on each of the armrests.

"I see you're following the instructions that came with the chair." She looked at him without getting up. "Well, one more painter bites the dust. I'll line the shelves with my art history term papers. Except I don't got shelves. Hey, you do—want some shelf paper? Hey, Keith, you wanna maid? A personal valet? An interior decorator? Expert landscaping?"

Not a crease appeared on his face. She wasn't too worried about what he saw when looking at her: a mop of ordinary brown hair, Italian olive skin, thick eyebrows, substantial features, a gash mouth. But Keith should've been more than ordinary. His skin apricot-colored; his hair dark, so straight, too fine, strands soft and separate as though he combed each by itself. His brow was intense, his eyes not darker than his skin, with only a slight bulge of weariness beneath each. His neck was long, his only flaw a strawberry mark under one sleek jawbone where he cradled his violin.

He got up, went into his music room, and came out with his violin. He held it to his ear, plucking and tuning it, staring vaguely at Charmaine. But his face did become even more colorful next to the instrument, glowing like the varnished wood, cared for—even loved by the doting violin. Charmaine's stomach growled.

"You're still at it, huh?" she said.

"Yes."

"You really still practice?"

"Of course."

"What for?"

"Auditions." He strummed the strings softly. "I've got one next week, and one a month after that, all winter."

"All planned like a train schedule: practice on your way to an audition, then practice on the way to the next."

"Something like that."

"Well, I quit today." She kicked her legs up and stared at her feet in black socks high above her face, raining grains of sand into her eyes. "That ever occur to you?—quitting and trying something more satisfying."

He resined his bow. "I've got to practice, Charmaine." His eyes were lazy. She recognized the look of drowsy love a musician has for his instrument. She said, "I can't stand the sight of my paints and brushes anymore." Once, long ago, she'd seen him play the instrument like a lover; he made it moan with pleasure and called it music. Musicians were funny, married to their instruments. An artist, though, had to try to create a new lover every time the hunger was great enough—not an artistic tribute to love, nor the expression of love in acrylics, nor an oil-based appreciation of love, nor a watercolor rendition of the sound or look or feel of love—but the lover himself.

She watched Keith rub the violin's wooden body with a soft cloth, poking his fingers under the strings to clean away all the resin powder. He tucked the chin rest under his jaw, the fiddle snug against his neck. "Please, Charmaine."

"I'm hungry, okay, Keith?"

"I'm going to practice."

". . . A banquet, a small feast . . ."

"You've got to go."

She kneeled on the couch, separated the cushions, looking for lost change. "I always figured it was your wife who gave you that hickey on your neck." She put her shoes on and went home.

At six the next morning she stood in his hallway and kicked on his door.

Keith actually wore pajamas, plain, pale blue trimmed with white. Charmaine went straight to his music room, deposited her easel and one fresh canvas, went back for her paints and brushes, one last trip for her paper bag of clothes, which she gave to Keith. "Put these in the bedroom, please." Then she took a shower. When she came out, wearing the same clothes, her hair in tight wet curls, she found him drinking coffee in the kitchen, her bag of clothes on the corner of the table.

"Oh, okay. I'll put them away myself."

"Charmaine, wait—"

"You're not going to be able to wear those pajamas, Keith."

"What?"

"Not while I'm doing you into a portrait."

"But—"

"And you won't be allowed into my new studio, either. That's where the canvas is. But you won't need to pose for me. A lot of my work can be accomplished wherever you are."

"I thought you quit painting."

She smiled. "Maybe you've inspired me. The way

you coax music out of that thing of yours." But she wouldn't be squeezing art out of herself—out of her wet insides like tubes of paint. She would paint him with her hands in his colors; no brush strokes, just fingerprints.

"I have to practice, Charmaine. That thing and I have an audition in four days."

"That's okay." She leaned down and kissed his cheek. Hesitated, then kissed his mouth, tasting the coffee. "Take another sip." He did, and she sucked it out of his mouth.

Keith said, "I'm not practicing."

"I noticed."

"The audition is in three days."

She lay on the couch, her head in his lap. His stomach buzzed against her ear when he spoke.

"I'm going to have to practice soon."

"Of course." She hooked a hand on the back of his neck, yanked his mouth down to hers.

"I think I'll eat before practicing. You hungry?"

"Yes." She opened her mouth against his throat.

"Wanna eat here or go out?"

"Neither."

"Charmaine, I've never seen you eat."

"Well, I do." She sat up, straddled his legs, chewed on his mouth. Holding his lower lip in her teeth, she said, "You always were so damn dedicated."

"Because I eat?"

She let his lip snap back. "Remember in the library, we really weren't studying together, it was a contest, to see who lasted the longest."

He checked his watch. "It's getting late. I probably shouldn't eat first."

"And you won. I can look real serious sucking a pencil. But really, you won."

"They have a brutal audition list for this one."

"You probably already have it memorized."

"Not quite."

"You must've practiced that thing half your life."

"I wish."

She pressed her nose against his. "Lemme see your tongue." He stuck it out and she bit it. "I'm painting you, ya know."

"I was wondering what you were doing."

"You're organic. Some paint isn't."

They were talking into each other's mouths. "You know," he said, "there'll probably be fifty people showing up to audition for one opening."

"I remember I missed your senior recital."

"I want to at least make it to the finals."

"I always wondered if you missed me, but Bertha was probably there cheering wildly." She licked the roof of his mouth.

"Her name was Betty. I'm gonna practice soon."

"But you worked so hard for it, and we were buddies."

"I know they'll ask to hear the Tchaikowsky first."

"I admit, Keith, I missed the recital on purpose." She rubbed her front teeth against his.

"Auditions can drive me crazy—I may try to practice the whole time before my turn."

"Engine engine number nine. . . ."

"Or I can stand around socializing with the people I'm competing with and worrying about whether the audition room is too hot or too cold."

"Going down the county line. . . ."

"I've gotta be able to run through that sonata like pouring honey. So they can't stop me."

"If the train goes off the track. . . ."

"They'll do that, you know, wave you aside right in the middle."

"Will you want your money back?"

"Tell me to practice."

Their mouths stuck together. He shut his eyes; Charmaine watched. With one hand he held her bushy hair behind her head.

While Keith slept for a few hours on the couch, Charmaine went into the studio-music room. She set her paints up, but left the caps on. She put the canvas on the easel. She took a break to look through the closet for the paintings she might've given him. She found a cake of resin in the pocket of every jacket and coat.

Later on, as soon as she heard his bow touch the strings, Charmaine came out of the studio. He had shut himself in the bedroom to practice. When she opened the door, he stopped. "Go on, I need to watch you," she said.

"I thought you were working."

"I am."

He played a note, and she put her hands under his arms. "Go on, Keith, practice, I need to feel how tight your muscles are."

"For a painting?"

"What else would I be doing?"

She put one hand on his shoulder, reached down and clamped the other in his crotch.

"What're you doing?"

"Measuring. Go on—play."

He raised the violin again. Charmaine kneeled at his feet, ran her hands down the outside of his legs from his hips to his knees. "I wish you'd take your pants off. I can't paint you through jeans."

He laid the violin on the bed and stepped out of his pants. "Now will you let me practice?"

"The shirt too."

In underwear and socks, he put the violin back under his chin. He was playing his warm-up: long notes, full bow, plenty of vibrato. He played three of them while Charmaine kneeled quietly behind him. He stopped when she put her hands on the insides of his thighs.

"Keep going, Keith. I have to get it right."

He poised the violin, hesitated.

"Go on, Keith." She kneeled like a spring at his feet, staring at his legs. The bow touched the strings and squawked when she put her face against the back of one leg. "Charmaine, what—"

"I hafta *test*—to see how much of you vibrates when you play."

The phone rang.

"Who would be calling you, Keith? You don't know anyone else."

He went to answer it, so Charmaine went back into the studio. She looked at her canvas—then switched it from vertical to horizontal. His footsteps finally whispered past the door. When she heard him pluck each string on the fiddle, then tune by bowing two strings together, she slunk down the hall, crept into the bedroom, dropped down on all fours and crawled up behind him. Stopped, crouching there. The floor vibrated. She rose. Barely an inch away, she stood quietly at his back, staring at his shoulder which moved as he bowed. She swayed slightly so his bow arm wouldn't bump her. Then she bit him, a wet phantom kiss, on the tip of his shoulder blade. Keith yelped, the violin squirted high in the air and landed on its back on the bed.

"I'm being quiet as I can, Keith. But I gotta know how your back muscles work while you play."

"Paint it from the front."

She shrugged. "If you say so." She dropped to the floor again, sat waiting while he picked up the violin, peered inside, and checked it all over.

"What took ya so long on the phone?"

"I ate an apple."

"Didja leave me the seeds at least?"

"You can have a whole apple if you want."

When he started to play, she kneeled upright, pressed her ear to his stomach. He managed one scale. "Are you stopping again? I'm listening for the apple."

He sat on the bed, the violin and bow beside him. "Charmaine, maybe I'd better tell you the musical facts of life."

Still on her knees, she stumped over to him, put her hands on his legs and leaned forward. "Is this gonna be like 'The Little Engine that Could'?" She pushed her hands up his thighs, up to the elastic of his underwear. "I think I can, I think I can, I really think I can." Keith held her shoulders, looking at her. She wiggled her fingers into his underwear, singing, "And you can do most anything, if you just think you can."

Keith fell over sideways on the bed, missing the violin but breaking the bow in half.

At dusk he went into the bathroom, showered, shaved. Clouds of violet-tinted steam came from under the door. Charmaine was still sitting on the floor. She watched him return.

"You sure have everything, Keith, pajamas *and* a bathrobe."

"I even have another bow. I don't have another Thursday afternoon."

He sat down to dry his feet. He dried between each of the toes on one foot, then began the other. Charmaine licked all his toes, and he dried them again.

"Hungry?" Keith asked.

"Nope." She sucked the stickiness off each of her fingers. "I'm happy about your progress."

"I didn't practice all day."

"The portrait—you're going to be beautiful."

He put the violin away and then dressed. "Can you fry me an egg?"

"I know how to mix paint."

He looked at her. They never spoke of his visit to her garage. "Never mind."

Before dawn she kneeled at his bedroom window, her chin on the sill, naked, shivering. The metallic sky opened up and bled, oozing water. She could not see the drops sparkling as they fell, nor the lines of liquid whips. No thunder and lightning broke. Only a heavy excuse for rain. It was a watercolor wash background, just wet.

The sheets rustled behind her. She didn't turn. She rested her pinched butt on her heels, pressed her knees together. Keith's feet thumped on the floor. "Charmaine. . . ." He sat beside her, passed his hand down her back. "You're all bones."

"We had to learn the skeletal system in anatomy class."

"You're freezing. You've got to drink something warm."

"Okay."

His mouth was wet and slick and hot. He put his bathrobe over her. "The train leaves at eight."

"Engine engine number nine. . . ."

Keith got dressed and put some extra clothes in a small suitcase.

"It's going to be a pretty day," Charmaine said.

"It's raining, isn't it?" Keith folded a pair of underwear.

"There could be a rainbow." She knew dampness changed the mood of a string instrument.

He carried his music folder and violin case. The suitcase hung from Charmaine's arm and bumped against her knee. They sat in red velvet seats. Charmaine's hair was wild from the dampness, and Keith said it tickled his face, so he found a rubber band and fastened it back for her.

Keith was asleep when breakfast was served, his violin case held tightly between his legs, the music folder clutched at his side. Charmaine ignored the breakfast announcement. The window was drippy and cold. She opened it a crack. Kneeling on her seat, she pushed her tongue out the window and caught a few drops of rain. The edge of the window was dirty and she crunched grit in her teeth. Keith slept with his mouth open. The music folder was easy to slide out from under his arm. One by one she slipped the sheets of music out the window. The wind whisked them away. The folder went out last. Keith held her hand and continued to sleep.

There was no rain on the trip home. He was out of the running in the symphony audition within the first hour. They boarded the train at noon on Saturday, after Keith checked the lost-and-found for his music folder. He held the violin case across his lap. "I didn't plan it this way," he said.

"Engine engine number nine. . . ."

"Not that I expected to win the very first one."

"Going down the county line. . . ."

"Stop it," he snapped.

Later on, Keith went to the dining car alone. When he came back, he stood in the aisle a moment, holding onto the luggage rack with both hands, looking down at Charmaine. Then he fell into his seat. "This won't happen again."

"You mean you're finally quitting?" She licked her lips.

"Of course not."

He slept the rest of the way home while Charmaine looked out the window. The sky was clear black. The train raced under a big dumb staring moon.

Keith took the elevator and Charmaine climbed the stairs alone. She was waiting at his door. He carried both the suitcase and the violin. He put his clothes away. The bed was still unmade, sheets trailing onto the floor. Charmaine went into the music room, then came back out. Keith came from the bedroom.

"I want to see the portrait."

"Didn't I give you some paintings once?"

"C'mon, I want to see what you've got so far."

"I can remember those pictures, but I might've forgotten to actually paint them."

Holding her arm, he opened the door and took her into the music room. The easel's back was to the door. The paints were covered. The brushes clean. No dabs of color had dripped on the floor. He walked around the easel, taking her along. She leaned against him.

"Beautiful, Charmaine." He looked at the clean canvas.

"I looked in the closet. I couldn't find those paintings. Did I forget to paint on them—did I give you blank canvas by mistake?"

He hesitated by the door. "You wanna eat before you go home?"

She shook her head. "I have painted with colors, Keith. But so many colors—color on color—it always turned black."

She took her paints and easel and the canvas back to her garage.

On his end, she knew the phone was screaming. She held her breath. His voice was low, unfrightened: "Hello."

"It's me."

"Okay. . . ."

"I've been painting, Keith, I really have—really, I'm trying. I've worked all night."

"What time is it?"

"Three. But Keith, there's no color, the paints aren't working, nothing goes onto the canvas. Nothing comes off the brushes. I threw the whole jar of black, it hit and splatted all over, but nothing on the canvas."

"I'm very tired. I have to get up early to practice."

"I threw *every* jar, Keith, they all cracked right against the canvas, there're puddles of color all over the floor. Nothing on the canvas. It's still blank."

"Who is this?"

She waited, wiping spittle from her chin.

"I'm sorry I called you. I'm sorry I tried to wake you."

"Okay."

She left the phone booth. Sitting on a box in front of the blank canvas, she pictured the planned portrait: Keith's Night. One train in a dark tunnel, sleeping there, black and glossy, eyes glowing drowsily. And here comes another train, screaming out of the night, fire in the control room, teeth bared as it races head-on into that same tunnel on a single track. Moments before impact. Unwilling art: The collision will never happen.

With a razor blade, she sliced the webbing between her thumb and index finger, on both hands. The blood came in weak trickles. She waited until it filled her cupped palms. Then she pressed her hands against the white canvas and squeezed, kneading it. Blood oozed up her arms, dripped from her elbows. She stopped and looked at her painted skin. The canvas remained untouched.

Animal Acts

Voice Over

Are you still unadulterated? Can you still ignore the tricks, the sleight-of-hand or juggling, and all the rest of the gala presented for your benefit by the girls in your circle? You need to realize that to gain the attentions of a dedicated man, even for one ceremonious hour, is their sought-for proof of beauty and desirability, a demonstration of their talent.

Setting. A party in Los Angeles: the living room of a patron of the Philharmonic. Minimal props—couch flanked by several chairs, circular arrangement. In the center: a coffee table with party food.

Sunday evening following the Philharmonic's matinee. Several guests are dressed in tails and white tie or floor-length black dresses, indicating they are musicians. Some of the other guests are in glittering gold or silver tuxedos or gowns: the patrons. There is one ordinary red-nosed clown and one costumed pink cow who has to hold her wine glass between papier-mâché hooves. The guests, as they enter, will stand or sit in a casual arrangement.

Low conversation; specific words inaudible. An occasional moo.

Stage directions. Enter the NARRATOR, *female dressed in workman's coveralls. Nondescript plain brown hair in no particular style. Empty-handed. She spots* ANTONIO, *standing slightly behind the couch, listening to the conversation of a few musicians, but not participating nor contributing. He is a blond Italian, wearing off-white slacks and jacket, a light-blue pinstriped shirt. A large man, but trim.*

VOICE OVER

Antonio is a conductor of small orchestras. Several years earlier the narrator played third trumpet under his direction in San Bernardino, and hasn't seen him since. To tell the truth, he doesn't remember her.

Stage directions. The NARRATOR *cuts through the party, people step aside for her, even the two musicians* ANTONIO *has been listening to. She steps right between them.* AN TONIO *takes one step back. The* NARRATOR *is between him and the rest of the party. Toe-to-toe.*

NARRATOR

I have to warn you about Randi.

ANTONIO

Excuse me?

NARRATOR

Just listen, it's very important. A matter of honor or degradation.

Antonio

I'm not sure I know—

Narrator

Yes, that's why I need to warn you.

Voice Over

He was older. He'd thickened. Not so much in girth, but in the skin on his face, like leather swollen with rain then stiffened in the sun. He'd conducted one small-time symphony after another, from San Bernardino to Albuquerque to Little Rock. Always the same lean sweeping style, power in his arms which made the brass respond, believing they were in Cleveland or Chicago, but their clams and pitch told otherwise. And also still the same—the fleeting look he would give with one bold eye to the musicians who missed entrances or cracked notes. Except for the few times someone earned his smile, for quality performances, or courageous ones. Never for the cheap ones. Like Randi's.

He'd come to Southern California again for his new position in Riverside, but without a girl on his arm tonight—that striking wife who is a doctor and beautiful, and therefore seems to make him all the more desirable.

Narrator

I've known I had to tell you this since I first saw her, during those two years I lived in New York playing the shows. Now I record jingles for commercials, you know.

But you just listen, because so far you've only known the silly amateurs, their props and costumes. They practice for hours alone in closets. But Randi's act can't be done alone, can't be rehearsed, is always live and has never yet failed because she's the one who gets the volunteer from the audience, and you could be next. Just imagine the marquee: The Great Antonio, featuring *Randi.* Is that what you call success? She will.

ANTONIO

You mean someone who's here tonight?

NARRATOR

Just listen—

VOICE OVER

It's been hard, he must've had years of coquettish pageantry, yet remained untouched. His age sits well with him. Yes, still those good looks, which gave him charm and happiness and every personal perfection, including fidelity like a diamond, hard so it would never crack, yet clear, so the whole world could look in at him. He had some talent too, and perhaps some heartbreaks, which never stopped him.

Stage directions. A few of the people on the close end of the couch turn toward the NARRATOR *and* ANTONIO, *watching and listening. A few of the standing guests also come closer, quietly waiting and listening. The volume of the other buzzing conversations lessens considerably.*

The NARRATOR *reaches offstage and is handed a microphone.*

She addresses ANTONIO:

NARRATOR

You just listen and perhaps you'll always be thankful you never made it to New York where you would've come across Randi, the girl I'm going to tell you about. Maybe once, long ago, she did start as a starry-eyed young thing dreaming of the stage. She managed to catch on in a few choruses, way off Broadway, but she was always around, at the parties and in the circle, because she let Clarence think he was catching on with her, and he knew everyone, one way or another, from freelancing, I guess. He played electric guitar—what else—and he called himself a musician because an amplifier made him loud and the part said "improvise."

Well, Randi'd already had a kid, who she'd given up for adoption sometime before I ever saw her, and an abortion, which I never knew about until afterwards, when she told us all about it at a fondue party on the Upper West Side. I guess if it weren't for Randi, I'd never know how an abortion can hurt like hell, sometimes worse than giving birth, but doesn't stink as bad.

VOICE OVER

During the concert that afternoon, he may've been deciding whether or not to try that Mahler symphony with his new group. He would have to consider personnel—the second bassoon he didn't have or the horn player he knew couldn't cut the part. Important thoughts, accompanied by the Philharmonic, about his upcoming season, how to make it his biggest yet, and yet do it all with the local talent—school music teachers and housewife musicians—he would be given to work with.

Mostly his age showed in and around his mouth and the corners of his eyes. He used to seem almost giddy backstage before a performance in San Bernardino. But in those days, New York, Cleveland, Philly, Chicago—they were all in front of him.

Narrator

The gathering, the circle, was usually pit musicians and a few people from the chorus seated around a platter of crackers and cheese or chips and dip. Randi always arrived starving and immediately began to load clam dip on wheat crackers, or she dipped her hand right into the bowl of avocado and sucked the lumpy green blobs from the tips of her fingers. Sometimes saliva ran down her chin, tinted white or green or even red, if there was chili sauce. And in between mouthfuls she would talk, and belch, and spit into ashtrays, and hiccup, and spray mouthfuls when she laughed, and fart then fan the air behind her ass—to share it, she said. And she would talk about shit and piss and snot and puddles of puke her cat left around her apartment; and cum, or spunk, as she called it—she talked about the texture of it when rubbed between her fingers or swished around her mouth. She demonstrated how to "chew" it once, with a mouthful of onion dip, then she opened her mouth so everyone could see how the creamy dip had liquified and coated her mouth and made murky bubbles when mixed with saliva. She offered to share it with someone, and no one volunteered, so she made Clarence try it and spit some into his mouth.

Stage directions. Enter a pirate who removes his wig at the door and an elephant who removes his green derby hat. The cow begins doing some soft-shoe alone in a corner.

NARRATOR

Then when the laughs died out, Randi might find the pet of whoever owned the apartment, hopefully a male dog, because, she said, she kept a file in her head of the appearance of their balls. Some were tight and neat and pink; others, she'd noticed, were baggy and/or crusty and blackish. But once—no, more than once—someone had a female cat, and Randi said, "Oh good, we can rub her pussy and make her yowl," then turned to a man—any of the men there, she seemed to know without hesitation which one she would choose—and said, "You do it—I know you know how." The guy would smile but never deny it, and the girl next to him would blush, but when Randi "knew" something like that, you can bet she really, personally, knew.

Stage directions. A peacock enters, a gorilla on his arm. It's a girl gorilla, who takes her head off and has long blond hair. The elephant juggles bowling pins and the clown pulls paper flowers out of his sleeve. Just a few of the original guests still hold private conversations, but most of them, and the cow, who has stopped dancing, press closer to the NARRATOR.

NARRATOR

She had a freckly face and a sharp nose and small eyes set close together. And she got plenty of men to do the act with her. Once one of the guys was talking about the way he would play the lead, if he had it, and Randi told him he might as well daydream about simultaneous orgasm. Wait, this one's even better: A guy was talking about how he'd impressed a certain music director when he was called to sub and learned the whole book in one night, and Randi was listening seriously, attentively, then she said, "Are you still doing it in the missionary position?" Wait a second, I'm not finished—

Stage directions. ANTONIO *has been taking side steps, moving behind the couch toward the other side of the party, but the* NARRATOR *also moves sideways, parallel to him, and they remain face-to-face. The already listening guests continue to watch the* NARRATOR, *although she has moved to the other side of the party with* ANTONIO, *where more guests abandon their own conversations to listen. They shush the peacock, who has started a mating call and dance. He says, "Oh!" and also turns toward the* NARRATOR.

The microphone whistles and the NARRATOR *clutches it to her chest with a sheepish smile. The mike picks up her heartbeat. Slightly rapid and very irregular.*

NARRATOR

Wait, because there are some things about Randi you still need to know. I just told you the background. Men seemed to find her irresistible, so I thought you should know. You—who were never jostled in a crowd, even at rush hour. An admirable skill—but not good enough.

Stage directions. Giggling, the NARRATOR *bumps* ANTONIO'S *arm and spills wine on his light-colored jacket.*

NARRATOR

You see, I just want you to be careful and not prize your fidelity too lightly because Randi's tricks always worked. A party was always sort of dull—like this one—until Randi arrived. The circle would just sit and talk about the performance that night, or other performances other nights, or other productions, or why they'd left whichever symphony orchestra they'd come from—except Clarence because he played electric guitar. Maybe once some orchestra somewhere hired him in the summer when they played highlights of rock 'n' roll adapted for strings and winds, and they called in an electric guitar from the union book for flavor, to make it realistic.

Then Randi would come in, dressed as always in faded jeans and a huge man's shirt stained with wall paint, her favorite shirt ever since her own painting party when a gang of guys she knew helped to paint her apartment. And I mean a *gang*. Then the only thing to wait for was someone to say, "How's tricks, Randi?" because she always had an answer.

A lot of times she had a new voice teacher to tell about, and she usually began with what he looked like without clothes, his posture when naked, and how he smelled.

"Which reminds me," she said once in a stage whisper to the girl in the circle next to her. "Every time I pass your husband I smell B.O.—and I like it!"

Stage directions. Several more people enter, most dressed as animals, one a giraffe on stilts. The clown begins to walk on his hands. Someone steps on his knuckles and says, excuse me, to his feet, then quickly turns back to the NARRATOR. *A horse enters in two parts. Each quickly drinks a glass of wine, then the hindquarters bends over and fuses itself to the head section. The horse tap dances. Both pairs of the horse's legs can jump and click heels in the air. Then someone, hurrying across the party toward the* NARRATOR, *goes right through the horse and breaks him in half again.*

NARRATOR

But I thought I'd better describe her entrances and her cues because it all depended on what the setting was at each party, although only she knew how to read the conditions, talentless as she was for musical theater. I saw her audition once, from the pit; her voice was shrill and she minced about on stage like an elf in pointy shoes.

Stage directions. Holding the microphone between her knees, the NARRATOR *puts one hand inside her shirt, across her body, under her armpit, flaps her other elbow up and down creating a fleshy popping sound, which gains the attention of the last of the original guests not already listening. Also of a bear walking on a beach ball, who, because he can't stand still, circles the knot of listeners, pressing close to the* NARRATOR *and* ANTONIO.

When she speaks again to ANTONIO, *she hooks an arm around his neck, bringing him close, only the microphone between her lips and his ear. If* ANTONIO *did not hold onto the* NARRATOR *by her waist, he would surely fall over.*

NARRATOR

Maybe it's even more important now for me to be sure you know about Randi, with you starting your new position. Like I say, someday after all the acts, you'll see the grand finale: tricks, spoofs, and marvels like you've never seen, and you've got to remember to remain unimpressed, as you always were.

VOICE OVER

In many ways, he was like wine, the finest wine—to someone who knows little about it—expensive, cool in a slender bottle; clear, bright color.

NARRATOR

At one party there was a dog which sniffed each and every person's knee, and I watched him go around the circle, to everyone in turn. No one seemed to notice, or someone may've moved a hand away if it was within reach of the dog's nose. When he got to me, I patted his smooth brow. Each time I stopped, thinking my turn was over, he pushed his nose under my hand, nudging me, and I kept patting. Until Randi came in, and the dog turned toward the opened door, then leaped over the circle to greet her. She let him stand up against her, his front paws on her shoulders, and everyone watched. She said, "Oh—does he do tricks?"

"Ignore him," the owner said. "Get down, Animal. He's just trying to get attention."

"Animal—great name for a dog," Randi said. She stepped into the circle to take some cheese off the platter, stuck her tongue out and slapped the slice of cheese there. She looked around the circle, and there were no empty seats, so she kneeled right there, at the buffet table, in the middle of the ring. "A guy I knew once had this real neat dog," she said. "He was in commercials because of this trained dog of his, and only he could command him, so he acted in commercials. He was going to get me a spot too, but I didn't see him again."

Stage directions. A lion roars through a speaker in his plastic nose. A sword swallower is eating olives from the tip of his sword, pushing them down his throat, then bringing the blade out clean. He has an accident, and the tip of the sword comes out his pants. A big parrot has a little dummy of a man on his shoulder. The gorilla has been blowing up balloons and twisting them into animal shapes. As she finishes each, she tosses it into the crowd clustered around the NAR-

RATOR, *all jockeying for a better view or to be able to hear more easily. The balloons lie underfoot, are kicked occasionally, sometimes stepped on and popped.*

NARRATOR

This is one of the reasons I'm telling you. I always thought fidelity was a talent like that to you. You know, loyal, man's best friend, whatever.

"That dog loved me," Randi said. "The guy said it was weird, because he was such a one-man dog, but he kept sitting up for me and wanting to shake hands. Can you imagine—kissing a man while shaking his dog's hand?" She made a little layer of cheese, salami, and another cheese and put it onto her tongue. She tried to roll her tongue into her mouth, like an elephant bringing in its food. It was an awfully big mouthful, but she went on with the story anyway.

"When we were on the bed," she said, "we couldn't seem to keep the dog off. He wanted to lie right between us, of course, first licking my face and then the guy's. It could've been fun, you know? Maybe I wasn't drunk enough. So the guy told the dog to sit in the bedroom doorway, and he told him to stay. He was a trained dog, so that's what he did." She gestured a lot, when she wasn't picking up more food. Not expressive gestures, necessarily. Sometimes she just picked spilled crumbs out of the rug while telling something. I noticed the wine in Randi's glass was cloudy, crumbs at the bottom from drinking with her mouth full, and I thought of you—glad you weren't there. Yes, glad you never made it to New York.

Stage directions. When the NARRATOR *stops to drain the last drop of wine from* ANTONIO'S *glass, he takes this opportunity to wipe his ear with one hand. The clown hands him a dotted handkerchief. Two white doves fly out of it. But when the* NARRATOR *continues speaking,* ANTONIO *drops his hand and has to hold onto her again. The difference in their heights makes this mouth-to-ear position difficult for him, but he doesn't seem to be complaining.*

NARRATOR

Well, Randi changed her position, so she was sitting flat on her ass with her legs in front of her.

Whenever I saw Randi at parties, I would think of you and pretend you were with me, as though you were seeing it firsthand, so you would be prepared. But I also always knew I would have to tell you about her myself someday, so I had to watch her for both of us.

"Like an audience," Randi giggled. "That dog watched us on the bed. He never panted either, that dog. Just stared. I wouldn't've minded so much if he would've panted a little, would've been more normal somehow."

The host went into the kitchen to refill the trays, so Randi waited for more food and ate a few crackers while she waited. Crumbs always spilled from the corners of her mouth.

"Anyway," she continued, "I don't know how far along we were, you know—who keeps track? But the dog, he jumped on the bed again. I think the guy had groaned or something. And the dog jumps up there and bites me! Right on the boob. I could show you the bite mark."

Someone said, that's okay, Randi. She had already been pulling her shirt up. "No? Okay. Well, some other time." She reached for some carrot sticks and dragged her sleeve through the bean dip. Really, it's hard to imagine her at one of *your* parties, I know. I used to hear people talking about times at your house after concerts, the spread your wife put out, the music, the view from your picture window.

Randi wasn't finished, though.

Stage directions. The NARRATOR *looks around, spots an empty chair, hooks it with one foot, and drags it over; she sits* ANTONIO *down and mounts his lap, facing him, crosses her ankles around the back of the chair.* ANTONIO *smiles. He takes a dish of peanuts and feeds them to her, popping them into her mouth with his fingers. The elephant exits in a huff. The rest of the party is absolutely silent. Then the* NARRATOR *laughs out loud, into the microphone.*

VOICE OVER

He was never sure who it was, in San Bernardino, who sometimes blared the notes too loud and made him look—and did make him wince, at least.

NARRATOR

Probably this time more than others, I tried to imagine Randi saying this with you in the circle, maybe telling it right to you alone, with the rest of us watching. And I tried to picture the way you would look or answer. Maybe the way your eyebrows rose when the flutes were flat, or the small smile you wore to deceive the audience when you bowed. Or maybe no way I ever saw you before.

"So I told him," Randi went on, "I thought he ought to kill it, you know, to avenge my honor."

Listen to this, are you listening?

Randi said, "We tied the dog's legs with my shirt. I think I put my underwear on him too, but I was drunk, you know, so I'm not sure. And he blindfolded the dog. We had him across the bed, right there with us, and I was getting impatient, you know, but he, the guy, wanted to do it right. I just remember laughing and laughing. He used a letter opener, it was all he had, and I caught the blood in two hands, very warm and smooth, and we used it for extra lubricant."

She popped a pickle slice into her mouth, and I could smell the juice of it.

Action. ANTONIO *stands, lifting the* NARRATOR *with him, her legs still wrapped around his waist. He walks to the couch, looks at the guests still seated there. They rise and back away. The guests begin to exit, by ones and twos, while* ANTONIO *lays the* NARRATOR *on the couch and begins to undress her. He does so in such a way that her body is never totally revealed. Strategically placed chairs—moved during the party—block the audience's view. When* ANTONIO *lies on top of her, no part of the* NARRATOR *is visible. The microphone picks up her breathing and heartbeat, and her stomach growls, but she has disappeared.*

When all the guests have exited, they gather in two groups in the wings and begin to applaud.

Finale. A trained dog enters walking on his hind legs. He passes the couch and is handed the microphone, which he then carries away as he exits. The passion on stage is in pantomime.

FICTION COLLECTIVE

BOOKS IN PRINT

	cloth	*paper*
The Second Story Man by Mimi **A**lbert	$15.95	6.95
Althea by J. M. **A**lonso	15.95	6.95
Searching for Survivors by Russell **B**anks	—	8.95
Babble by Jonathan **B**aumbach	15.95	6.95
Chez Charlotte and Emily by Jonathan **B**aumbach	15.95	6.95
The Life and Times of Major Fiction by Jonathan **B**aumbach	15.95	—
My Father More or Less by Jonathan **B**aumbach	15.95	6.95
Reruns by Jonathan **B**aumbach	15.95	6.95
Plane Geometry by R. M. **B**erry	16.95	7.95
Heroes and Villains by Jerry **B**umpus	16.95	8.95
Things in Place by Jerry **B**umpus	—	6.95
Ø Null Set by George **C**hambers	15.95	6.95
The Winnebago Mysteries by Moira **C**rone	15.95	6.95
Amateur People by Andree **C**onnors	15.95	6.95
Faithful Rebecca by Janice **E**idus	15.95	7.95
Take It or Leave It by Raymond **F**ederman	—	10.95
Coming Close by B. H. **F**riedman	15.95	6.95
Museum by B. H. **F**riedman	15.95	6.95
Temporary Sanity by Thomas **G**lynn	15.95	6.95
Music for a Broken Piano by James Baker **H**all	15.95	6.95
The Talking Room by Marianne **H**auser	15.95	7.95
Holy Smoke by Fanny **H**owe	15.95	6.95
In the Middle of Nowhere by Fanny **H**owe	—	8.95
Mole's Pity by Harold **J**affe	15.95	6.95
Mourning Crazy Horse by Harold **J**affe	15.95	7.95
Moving Parts by Steve **K**atz	10.95	—
Stolen Stories by Steve **K**atz	15.95	6.95
Find Him! by Elaine **K**raf	15.95	6.95
The Northwest Passage by Norman **L**avers	15.95	7.95
I Smell Esther Williams by Mark **L**eyner	15.95	7.95
Modern Romances by Judy **L**opatin	15.95	7.95
Emergency Exit by Clarence **M**ajor	15.95	6.95
My Amputations by Clarence **M**ajor	15.95	—
Reflex and Bone Structure by Clarence **M**ajor	—	7.95
Four Roses in Three Acts by Franklin **M**ason	15.95	6.95
Animal Acts by Chris **M**azza	18.95	8.95
The Secret Table by Mark **M**irsky	15.95	6.95
Encores for a Dilettante by Ursule **M**olinaro	15.95	6.95
When Things Get Back to Normal by Constance **P**ierce	15.95	7.95
Rope Dances by David **P**orush	15.95	6.95
Broad Back of An Angel by Leon **R**ooke	15.95	6.95

Spectator by Rachel **S**alazar	15.95	6.95
The Common Wilderness by Michael **S**eide	17.95	—
The Comatose Kids by Seymour **S**imckes	15.95	6.95
The Charnel Imp by Alan **S**inger	15.95	8.95
Fat People by Carol Sturm **S**mith	15.95	6.95
Crash-Landing by Peter **S**pielberg	—	7.95
The Hermetic Whore by Peter **S**pielberg	15.95	6.95
Twiddledum Twaddledum by Peter **S**pielberg	15.95	6.95
Matinee by Robert **S**teiner	21.95	10.95
The Endless Short Story by Ronald **S**ukenick	15.95	6.95
Long Talking Bad Conditions Blues by Ronald **S**ukenick	15.95	6.95
98.6 by Ronald **S**ukenick	15.95	7.95
Meningitis by Yuriy **T**arnawsky	15.95	6.95
Griever: An American Monkey King in China by Gerald **V**izenor	15.95	8.95
Agnes and Sally by Lewis **W**arsh	—	6.95
Uncle Ovid's Exercise Book by Don **W**ebb	18.95	8.95
Heretical Songs by Curtis **W**hite	15.95	6.95
Statements I	15.95	6.95
Statements II	—	6.95
American Made: New Fiction from the Fiction Collective	15.95	8.95

FICTION COLLECTIVE

c/o Department of English, Brooklyn College, Brooklyn, New York 11210